Knights of the Grail

Linda Proud
Knights of the Grail
Based on the legend of King Arthur

with illustrations by
Hayley Simmons

A STORYTELLER TALE
from
THE GOOD COMPANY FOR CHILDREN CO LTD

Storyteller Tales

Published by

The Good Company for Children Co Ltd
3 Parklands Close
off Fife Road
East Sheen
London SW14 7EH

Tel: 0181-876 0445   Fax: 0181-876 0173

First published by The Good Company for Children Co in 1995

ISBN 1-900197-02-2

Copyright © Linda Proud 1995

Printed by BPC Wheatons Exeter

Cover design
Quadrant Design Studios, 84 Long Lane, Borough, London SE1

Cover illustration
Hayley Simmons

Once upon a time...

STORYTELLING is as old as children. From the earliest days, mothers, fathers, uncles, aunts, grandparents and friends have set children on the lap and told tales which happened once upon a time.

The storyteller is an artist, painting pictures in the mind, leading the child across a canvas which bursts with colour at each turn of the story. For sheer fun for both adult and child, nothing can beat the telling of a thunderously good tale.

We at the *Good Company for Children Co Ltd* are delighted to be playing our part in rekindling the art of storytelling. In the process, our aim is to provide great enjoyment and educational value to all who meet our books.

We have tried to make the task of storytelling easier for both reader and listener alike. The books are divided into short episodes, and our hope is that both adult and child will want to carry on with the tale tomorrow. The italicised typeface helps the reader's eye move more easily to pick up the parts where the storyteller's voice would change with each character. Of course those with more practice at telling tales will know the value of silence between dramatic movements.

Storytelling is basically natural to every mother, father, 'aunt' and 'uncle'. Our reasons for publishing are to provide you with the best of company for yourself and children and, we hope, many hours of family happiness along the way.

DAVID BODDY
Publisher
Good Company for Children Co Ltd

The storyteller

MY NAME is Sir Bedivere, Knight of the Round Table and Cup-bearer to the glorious King Arthur. Such are my titles but, in truth, I am a simple man who likes simple things, especially animals.

During my time at the Round Table, I did not really fit in with the other knights, who loved nothing so much as to swap tales of romance and battles over mugs of ale. I was particularly embarrassed by the tales of romance.

You see, I am bluff and clumsy in such matters and avoid them when I can. Besides, I'm not the sort of chap the ladies fall for. Not mortal ladies, anyway. After all, when you have men such as Gawain, Lancelot and Tristan at your side, it is not really surprising to find yourself being overlooked.

I am much more at home when it comes to the Otherworld.

I do not know for what reason the Powers singled me out for especial favours, but Merlin the Wizard gave me the gift of being able to see things which are invisible to most. And so it was that, while my companions-in-arms were completely caught up in the affairs of this earthly world, I could see what it was that gave us our power, and what it was that took it away.

I have often come back to this world, to whisper my story in the ears of a poet. Always the poet interprets it in the light of his own age. But the true story is eternal. I do hope you enjoy it.

Guide to pronunciation

IN HONOUR of Arthur's origins in ancient Britain, some names in the story have been derived from Welsh, in particular that of Guinevere. The original name was Gwinhwyfar (Gwin-hooey-var) but for ease we have changed it to Gwinhavar.

Caerleon is easy to pronounce but its spelling may cause the reader to stumble. Therefore it has been changed to its closest equivalent in English — Carleon, as in Carlisle, though its correct pronunciation is Care-leon, as in Caerphilly.

The syllables underlined in the following should receive a slight emphasis:

Guinevere	*Gwin*-ha-va
Uther	*Oo*-ther
Gawain	*Ga*-wain
Isolda	E-*sold*-a
Lyonesse	Leo-*ness*
Caerleon	*Car*- or *Care*-leon

Contents

First day
A gift from the Goddess

SOMETIMES THINGS COME OUT OF NOWHERE. A dog came out of nowhere when another dog was walking along the road. The car came out of nowhere as the dogs raced yapping over the bridge. There was a squeal of brakes and then everything went quiet. People on the pavement shrank back, staring at the car and the hairy body of one dog beneath the wheels. No-one came forward. Everyone was too scared to move.

Suddenly a man ran forward from a long way back. He must have come from the meadow on the other side of the river. He raced over the bridge, shouting at the driver of the car: "Don't move!"

He fell to his knees and spoke to the dog, putting his big hands on its shivering body. "Move the car backwards, very slowly," he said to the driver.

The driver released the brakes and the strange man pushed the car off the dog.

The next thing anyone knew, the man had disappeared.

Now the road led to the huge meadow where people went for walks. One little boy with a very runny nose stood on the grass watching other children flying kites. No-one wanted to play with him because he was always sniffing.

He walked along wondering what had happened to that marvellous man who had rescued the dog. Much of the meadow was flooded from the winter rains. The little boy skirted the water's edge, thinking about the man from nowhere.

Then, by the bridge across the river, he suddenly saw the man again. The man was dressed very strangely, in a leather jerkin and woollen trousers. The man looked baffled, as if he wasn't quite sure where he was.

"Are you lost?" asked the little boy.

"I can't find my way back," said the mysterious man.

"I saw you rescue the dog. You were very brave," said the boy.

"It's my job to be brave. I'm a knight."

Well, the little boy had never met a knight before.

"What's your name?" he asked.

"Sir Bedivere."

"And where do you come from?"

The knight dropped his voice. "Can you keep a secret?"

The boy nodded.

"I come from another world."

"From space?" cried the boy.

"No, from a place that is now but not quite here. I did not intend to come back to this world, but I heard the dog in pain and I had to come. Now I can't find my way back."

"Where is this place?" the boy demanded.

"Not quite here. Just over there."

"Where's that?"

"I'm not sure," said the knight.

"How many people live there?"

"Lots."

"Human people?"

"Yes. There's me, and there's a king and a queen. But most of the others were born in the Otherworld and they have always lived there."

"Who is the king?" asked the boy.

"His name is King Arthur."

Now the little boy had heard of King Arthur and began to pepper the knight with questions.

"Very well," said Sir Bedivere, "I can see that I must tell you the whole Tale. But it is a long story, so you will have to come and see me every day and I'll tell you a little each time."

The man was very strange but there were lots of people about, flying kites and sailing boats, so the boy knew he would be safe. He went with the knight to the edge of the flooded meadow where they sat down to look at the sheet of water that stretched as far as they could see. The boy was very happy to have met a new friend, one who did not seem to mind about his sniffing.

Sir Bedivere began, speaking softly at first.

IMAGINE THAT IT IS NIGHT-TIME. All is dark here but not quiet. You can hear the water slapping on the shore and dragging the shingle away. And can you see the moon? It is big and full, there — straight ahead of us, just above the water. Then there is another moon, there on the water itself, moving with the waves, and its light runs towards us. Now look carefully. Do you see the boat? It has a square sail and on it is the picture of a long sword pointing downwards. The boat is coming this way. Behind us are dark cliffs and the beach is rocky. We are on the coast of Cornwall. And look, here on the beach ahead of us, watching the boat come in, is a man. He is not good-looking or well-dressed. His hair is long, so is his beard, and he wears a gown as dark as the night. He is a quiet man; someone who likes to be by himself.

Now the boat is close. There is a lady on board. Do you see her? She is the most beautiful lady you may ever have seen, more beautiful than a princess, taller than a queen. She has a little bundle in her arms.

The boat is sliding up on to the beach and crunching on the shingle. The man walks forward.

"Merlin," says the lady. *"Your prayers have been heard."*

"Goddess!" says the man called Merlin and he falls to his knees. *"Please help us. The Red Dragon is becoming too strong for us and Britain suffers."*

The Goddess says: *"You must find my sacred treasures: the hallows sword, the hallows spear and the hallows cup. While they are hidden, the people forget me. But first you need to restore the order of law and to stop the people fighting each other. They must become one people in one fair nation. For that you need a good king."*

"Britain has many kings," says Merlin, *"and not a good one amongst them."*

"Here is your good king," says the Goddess. And she holds out the little bundle to him. *"Take him, Merlin. Look after him well and raise him as a knight. He will be king in fifteen years."*

"What is his name?" asks Merlin.

"It is Arthur," says the Goddess.

Merlin looks down at the bundle and sees the face of a sleeping baby. When he looks up again, the boat is sailing back towards the moon in the water.

That is how it all began.

"Where were you when all this happened?" asked the boy.

"Now that's a good question," said Sir Bedivere. "We all have to find that out, who we are and where we came from. Now where was I when all this was going on? — Oh yes, I was at home in Normandy, which is a part of France."

I WAS BORN about the same time as Arthur but there was nothing special about me, apart from being the son of a king that is. And if you think that is special, I can tell you that in my day there were an awful lot of kings.

Well, being the son of a king, and of a queen of course, meant that I had to grow up to be a knight. There was no choice. Do you want to know what it takes to be a knight?

You have to exercise every muscle in your body until it is as big as a melon and as hard as a brick. You have to learn to ride a horse twice the size of any horse you might have seen, and the horse also has to have muscles as big as melons and as hard as bricks. But you can be as big and as strong as you can get and you still won't be a knight. That's because the thing which makes a knight is learning how not to be afraid.

Do you want to know about the lessons in bravery? First they put you in a dark dungeon that is oozing with stinking old water and you have to stay there and not move as spiders run over you. Then after the spiders come rats. Nibbling rats that bite your toes. After the rats come spiny things. It's too dark to see what they are, but they grunt and snort and dribble. But none of these things is really scary. What's really scary is the voices. Horrible voices which whisper and spit and tell you what other people think about you. Anyway, to cut short the story about my ordeals and my courage, I survived all these things.

One day my father called me to him. He said that although my muscles were big and strong, and although I was brave

KNIGHTS OF THE GRAIL

and fearless, there was yet something more a man must do to become a knight. *"What would that be, father?"* I asked.

He said: *"Bedivere, it is necessary that every knight must love a lady."*

"No!" I shouted. *"No! Never!"*

"It is necessary," said my father sternly, his face as long and as sharp as a sword.

"I'd rather live in that dungeon with the spiders, the rats and the spiny things!" I cried.

"Bedivere," my father shouted. *"You have no choice!"*

Then my mother had a word with me. *"Have you ever thought sweetly about any girl?"* she said. *"Someone like your cousin perhaps?"* My cousin was blonde, blue-eyed and absolutely horrible.

"I hate her!" I cried. *"I prefer the spiny things!"*

My mother and father kept on at me for hours. I sat in the corner with my fingers in my ears. It was such a commotion that I went to bed with my ears ringing. Then, the next morning, my father put me on a boat that was going to Britain.

"Britain is a festering rat hole!" he shouted. *"But it's too good for you!"*

SO THAT WAS HOW I CAME TO BRITAIN. I presented myself at the court of the Pendragon, that is, the king of all the kings of Albion. His name was Uther. I asked him how I could become a knight and he said that, although I was big and strong and fearless, I was a bit brutal. *"There's more to being a knight than brute strength,"* he said.

"I suppose you mean girls," I mumbled.

"Girls?" he said, surprised. *"What have they got to do with*

it? No, I mean you have to learn how to be sly and crafty. It's called the Art of War. One of my knights will teach you." So saying, he gave me over to the care of a man called Sir Hector.

So I went to live with Sir Hector and his wife. They had two children. One was a boy called Kay who was a year older than me. He was sixteen. The other was a boy my own age, someone who Sir Hector had also taken to train in the Art of War. His name was Arthur.

Suddenly Sir Bedivere fell quiet and looked to the west.

"The sun is going down now and we need to rest. Once a tale has begun, it must continue to its end. That is the law. Come back tomorrow and I'll tell you some more."

He looked at the boy who had a very runny nose and kept sniffling wetly. The boy's face was as hard as if someone had bitten his soul. But he looked up at Sir Bedivere with eyes as big as saucers because he had never met anyone so wonderful before. Sir Bedivere reached out and touched him gently on the head. "When you come back tomorrow," he said, "bring a hankie with you."

Day 2
Albion at war

IT WAS THE START of the school holidays so on the next day the sniffling boy rushed back to where he had met the mystery knight. Finding him sitting on a big stone by the river, the boy sat beside him, close enough to touch. He sniffled loudly.

"Where's your handkerchief?" asked Sir Bedivere.

"Sorry, Sir," said the boy, remembering that he was talking to a fearless knight. "I forgot it."

So Sir Bedivere took out his own handkerchief and gave it to him. It was made of beautiful Irish linen and embroidered in the corner was a picture of a metal helmet with a cat sitting on top.

The boy blew loudly into the handkerchief, several times. When his face came out of the linen, it was smiling and clean.

"Thanks," he said, giving the handkerchief back.

"You may keep it," said Sir Bedivere. "Now settle down. There is much more story to tell you."

ARTHUR HAD BEEN LIVING in Sir Hector's house for a very long time, about fifteen years. Arthur believed he was the son of Sir Hector and the brother of Kay. But Kay, who was a year older, said it was not true. He told me that Arthur was washed up on the beach when he was a baby and that an old wizard found him.

Arthur smiled at me. *"It's not true,"* he said. But he did not look a bit like Kay. Arthur's hair was the colour of autumn leaves and his eyes were the colour of the ocean. And, unlike Kay, who was big and strong, Arthur was slight. He had muscles but not like melons. *"Kay's always saying that I'm not his brother, but it's not true,"* said Arthur the day we first met.

"It is true!" said Kay. *"A dirty old wizard brought you here. You're from the fairy kingdom!"*

Arthur laughed again and shook his head. Whenever Arthur laughed, music seemed to play inside me. Tinkling music, the music of water.

EVERY DAY WE HAD LESSONS in the Art of War and Arthur was the best of us. He could be more sly and more crafty than anyone. He would think of a battle like a game of chess and plan it all out beforehand. He was good at taking people by surprise, pouncing on them and ambushing them.

Every day we had to put armour on. It was made of metal but not the kind of metal you know. It was soft like play dough. You could make it into any shape you liked, only once it had been made into a shape, it could not be made into any other shape. It was a special metal that was made by smiths who lived underground. They gave it to men in exchange for being left alone. We never saw them, but any time you came to a big grassy mound in the countryside, which had a door made out of stone, you would be sure to find a bucket full of soft metal waiting for you. What you had to do was to walk round the mound three times then stand at the door and say, *"Thank you Mr Smith and Mrs Smith, and thank you all the little Smiths. May you live in peace and never be troubled by Man."* Then you could take the bucket and get some armour made for you by the armourers.

The armour only fitted over our bodies. Our legs and arms were dressed in leather. But we had metal gloves and metal shoes and metal helmets. Kings and the chief knights wore special crests on their helmets, often in the shape of an animal such as a leopard or a dolphin or a pelican.

ALTHOUGH WE WERE NOT KNIGHTS YET, we fought in some battles. You see at that time the islands of Britain were at war with each other. The Scots were in Ireland, the Irish in Wales, the Welsh were in Albion and —

"Where?" said the boy.
"Albion," Sir Bedivere repeated.
"Where's that?"
"It's here," he said.
"But this is England."
"Albion is its true name," said Sir Bedivere. "Now let's get on."

The Welsh were in Albion, and the Albions were all over the place. There was a big battle at St Albans. The Scots and the Irish had banded together to kill off all the Albions. The battle was so fierce and so terrible that every day hundreds of knights were killed. So soon we began to run out of knights, and the boys in training were made to fight.

It was my first real battle. It was the first time that I set my spear on the front of my saddle and charged towards men who wanted to kill me. Was I frightened? What, after the spiny things and the horrible voices? No, of course I wasn't. I was thrilled. I charged in with Arthur and Kay beside me. Kay and I were tough and we hit the enemy like tanks, scattering them all over the place. But Arthur was crafty and set traps and trip wires and brought down many more men than we did.

Kay was knocked off his horse by one of the enemy. You

expect to come off your horse quite soon in a battle. Then you stand and fight with swords. Kay's sword clanged against the sword of his enemy. CLANG! CLANG! CLANG! Before long, Kay fetched the man such a blow that the man fell over backwards.

Kay roared with triumph and lifted up his sword to strike the man's head off his neck.

"*No!*" shouted Arthur.

"*What do you mean, 'no'?*" demanded Kay. "*If I don't kill him, he's going to kill me!*"

Arthur stood over the man on the ground.

"*What is your name?*" he asked him.

"*King Lot of Orkney,*" said the man, his voice as gravelly as dry oats. "*What is yours?*"

"*Arthur of Albion. This is Kay, my brother. Do you have any last request?*"

"*Only one,*" said the King of Orkney.

"*And what is that?*" said Arthur.

"*Please don't kill me!*" pleaded the king.

"*Very well,*" said Arthur. "*You may go free.*"

"*Are you MAD?*" shouted Kay. "*I haven't risked my life just to let him go free!*"

But Arthur was thinking ahead, and he persuaded Kay that it was a really good idea not to kill anyone who asked for mercy. "*You'll see,*" he said. "*He'll be on our side after this.*"

And so it turned out.

IN THE NEXT BATTLE, the men of Orkney fought with us against the rest of the Scots and Irish. King Uther Pendragon was so impressed with this trick that he had it

made an official part of the Art of War, and all over the
battlefield knights began to give other knights mercy, on
condition that they changed sides. So the armies of Albion
began to swell and grow big.

The kings of Scotland and Ireland gathered together to
talk about how the war was going. *"The Albions are getting
crafty,"* they said. *"So we must be crafty too."* And they
thought of a plan to kill King Uther.

Now there is good craftiness and there is bad craftiness.
Poisoning the leader of your enemies is against the rules of
the Art of War. But the Scots sent a spy into our camp who
put poison ivy into the well which supplied the king with
water. King Uther died that night, along with everyone else
who had water with his supper. The next morning the
Albions woke up to find that they had no leader and that one
hundred of their best knights were also dead.

The enemy armies, sure that they had won the war,
celebrated all night and then stayed in bed all the next day.

The Albions gathered together in the town of St Albans.
"It is the end of us!" they cried. *"King Uther had no child.
Who will be the next Pendragon?"*

But King Uther did have a daughter, called Morgana. She
was really annoyed. *"I am the lawful child of King Uther!"*
she said. *"I am the next Pendragon!"*

Well girls, of course, can't be kings, so the men just
ignored her, which made Morgana furious.

NOW WE HAD MANY KINGS to choose from, at least
eleven: the King of the North people, and the King of the
South People, the King of the West People and the King of
the East People, and then all the Kings of all the Middle

Bits. Each one of them wanted to be the Pendragon.

As each one of them hollered *"IT WILL BE ME!"*, so the other ten hollered *"NO IT WILL NOT!"*.

"It really OUGHT to be ME!" shouted Morgana, but no-one would listen.

"This is ridiculous!" shouted Sir Hector. *"The enemy armies will be up and about soon, and then they will attack us!"*

JUST OUTSIDE OF ST ALBANS on a hill there was a huge circle of tall, grey stones. They had been there forever and a day, which is much longer than St Albans had been there. Sir Hector ran to the stone circle, taking Kay, Arthur and me with him. He turned round three times then held up his arms in the air and shouted: *"Help! Help us!"*

Suddenly a kingfisher flew towards us like a flashing blue arrow. It swooped round the stones and landed on the largest one. Smoke came up from the ground and none of us could see each other. The smoke had a queer smell which was rather nice, like the smell of cakes baking. The mist soon cleared, as quickly as it had come, and in the place of the kingfisher stood an old man with long hair and a gown as dark as the night.

"Merlin," said Sir Hector. *"Thank God you've come!"* And he rushed forward to hug his old friend. Kay and I were astonished by everything, but Arthur ... Arthur had the strangest expression on his face. It was the kind of look which said: *"I don't know who you are, but I'm sure we've met before."* Merlin saw him staring and winked at him.

"Why did he wink at Arthur?" said Kay. *"Why didn't he wink at me? I'm the oldest!"* But Merlin took no notice of

Kay. He took Sir Hector to one side for a talk. The next thing we knew, that funny mist which smelt of marzipan was coming back, and the next thing after that, Merlin had disappeared and a kingfisher was flying away.

"We're all to go back into the town," said Sir Hector, looking much happier. *"Straight away. It's time to find out who the new Pendragon will be."*

·"That's all for today," said Sir Bedivere to the boy.

"Oh no!" he cried. "Please go on. I want to know who the new Pendragon is."

"But it's obvious,", said Sir Bedivere. "It's Arthur."

"Yes, I know," said the boy with a sniff. "But I want to know how everyone else finds that out."

"That I shall tell you tomorrow," said Sir Bedivere.

Day 3
The sword in the stone

WHEN THE BOY WENT TO THE MEADOW on the next day, at first he could not find Sir Bedivere.

"He's gone!" he thought. His big eyes filled with tears. But then he caught sight of the knight amongst some trees.

He ran to where Sir Bedivere was kneeling with his face pressed against the rough, grey bark of a willow. The boy thought he would creep up on the knight and surprise him. But it was the boy who got the surprise. For Sir Bedivere was talking to the tree! Then he stopped speaking and started to listen, as if the tree were talking back to him!

"Listen," said Sir Bedivere, into the tree. "I'll have to go now. He's here. What? Yes, of course, I'll call you tomorrow. Bye now." He turned to the boy.

"Who were you talking to?" the boy asked him.

"My folks back home. They're wondering where I've got to. But I told them that the Gate has closed. I told them that, since the tale has begun again, I cannot come home until it is finished. Now, where had I got to? Oh yes, I remember. We were in St Albans and everyone was shouting . . ."

"*IT'S ME!*" cried the King of the North People. "*I'm the new Pendragon!*"

"*No you're not, it's ME!*" cried the King of the South People.

"*No you're not, it's ME!*" cried one of the Kings of the Middle Peoples.

"*It's ME!*" cried the King of Cornwall.

And so all the kings cried: "*ME! ME! ME! ME!*"

"*It is not for us to decide who the new Pendragon is,*" said Sir Hector. "*We must all go to the church and pray to God for guidance.*"

Everyone agreed and they all went to church as Sir Hector suggested. They prayed long. They prayed hard. They knelt on their knees till their knees went numb. Each of the bad and greedy kings prayed the same prayer: *"Dear God, make ME the next high king. Please, oh please, make it ME."*

WHEN THEY HAD STOPPED PRAYING everything seemed the same as before. But outside the church there was a huge stone where no stone had been before. There, plump on the path leading to the church. It just appeared. As if out of nowhere.

The first man out of the church was not looking where he was going. He stumbled straight into the stone. *"Ouch! Who put this here?"* he demanded crossly. *"And who stuck this extraordinary sword in it?"*

For indeed a sword stood out of the stone, held only by its point. The sword was gold, encrusted with jewels, and it glowed with a strange light. The man wanted it badly, so he pulled at the sword but he could not budge it. He tried again and failed. Finally he put both feet against the stone and pulled hard with both hands. The sword was stuck fast.

"Well by my spurs, here's a mystery," he said.

He obviously could not read, for on the stone were letters of gold which said: *WHOEVER PULLS THIS SWORD FROM THIS STONE IS RIGHTWISE THE KING OF ALL BRITAIN.*

So here was a miracle, come in answer to our prayers. All the kings and knights crowded round the sword, pushing and shoving, wanting a chance to have a pull at it. The sword was so beautiful that everyone was grabbing at it.

Suddenly a mist arose and all the kings and knights froze

in what they were doing. In a slow, eerie sound, a voice came out of nowhere.

"A toournaaament must be arraaanged!" said the voice. Everyone remained stunned, then suddenly snapped back to life. Each king started to shout that he had just had a really good idea. *"Let's have a tournament!"* they all said together.

Now part of the training for a knight is a mock battle, and that is what a tournament is. In a tournament, everyone rides out to do battle in a field, but our spears and swords are blunted so that we don't kill each other.

SO IT WAS ARRANGED for all the knights and kings to fight each other, and for the winners to have a go at pulling out the sword from the stone.

Kay was sixteen and ready to become a knight so his father Sir Hector took out his sword and placed it on his son's shoulder and spoke the words of knighthood:

"Always be a good knight,
Always fight for what is right.
All the bad things hack and hew,
And to your king be true.

By the power of St Michael I make you knight. Arise Sir Kay!"

Now that he was a knight, Kay was eligible to fight in the tournament. The field was full of knights and kings riding at each other with spears and striking at each other with swords. Whoever won a round was given the chance to try and pull the sword from the stone. But though the sword was held only by its tip, no-one could pull it from the stone.

Kay rushed about the battlefield hacking and hewing.

Suddenly his sword broke and he had to come off the field. *"Arthur!"* he said, panting. *"Fetch me another sword!"*

Arthur ran off at once. He was like that, always ready to run about for people. The next thing we knew, he was back, sooner than any of us had expected. As he ran towards us flourishing the sword, he looked like St George or St Michael and ready to slay a dragon. The sword flashed with the colour of emeralds, rubies and diamonds.

"This isn't my sword," said Kay, a bit cross, and then again, a bit mystified. *"Where did you get it?"*

"It's the one from the stone," Arthur replied, shyly. *"I thought it would save time if I borrowed it. I can put it back later."*

Kay and I looked at him with astonishment. Then Kay grabbed the sword. *"Tell no-one of this,"* he commanded us, and then he ran to find his father.

"Sir," he said to Sir Hector, panting. *"Here is the sword from the stone. So it must be ME who is the new Pendragon!"*

Now although Merlin had told Sir Hector to expect the stone, he had not told him who the new king was. But Sir Hector had a pretty good idea that it was not his son, Kay.

"Rubbish!" said Sir Hector. *"Tell me the truth, Kay."*

It was the rule in Sir Hector's family never to tell lies, so Kay admitted the truth. *"Arthur pulled it out,"* he said, looking ashamed, as people do when they are caught out telling lies.

Sir Hector and the three of us went back to the church and Sir Hector made Arthur put the sword back in the stone. He then tried himself to pull it out. It was stuck fast. Kay tried. I tried. None of us could budge the sword.

Then Arthur stepped up and pulled at it. There was a

moment's resistance. He pulled again. This time it started to move, slowly, slowly, and then — TWANG! — the sword sprang free from the stone, ringing as if a bell had been struck.

Well, to say that we were astonished is to put it mildly. There we were, all striving to be knights, and the best warrior amongst us was Kay. To be honest, we thought that Arthur hardly had what it takes to be a knight, let alone a king. Let alone the Pendragon.

The bells of the great church were rung and everyone ran from the tournament field as fast as they could go. There was young Arthur, standing in front of them, putting the sword in the stone, and then pulling it out again, for all to see.

All the townspeople dropped to their knees and hailed Arthur as the new Pendragon. *"Arthur! Arthur! Arthur!"* they shouted.

But the kings and knights did not much like the idea of a fifteen year old boy being the high king, so they all had yet another go at pulling the sword from the stone. But of course they all failed.

SUDDENLY EVERYONE BECAME AWARE that an enormous dog had appeared amongst them. It was a big, grey Irish wolfhound. *"What is going on here?"* demanded the dog. Everybody jumped back in alarm.

"Whoops!" said the dog, *"Sorry, I forgot..."* Then a mist rose up. Then the mist went down, and Merlin stood in the place of the dog. Now everyone had heard of Merlin, but few had met him before. *"What is going on here?"* demanded Merlin.

"It seems that only this boy can pull the sword from the stone," they told him.

"Well, well, well," said Merlin, trying to sound surprised, for of course he had known all along who the new Pendragon was to be. *"Arthur, then,"* he said, *"will be our new High King."*

The older, stronger, more experienced kings muttered: *"Why should we be ruled by a boy?"*

As for Morgana, she stood and watched Arthur with the yellow eyes of a snake. But the ordinary folk were delighted.

Arthur himself had no knowledge of his origins and no ambition to be a king. He was embarrassed by all the kneeling and cheering.

"Take the sword, Sire," said Merlin, and winked at him.

With that wink, something stirred in Arthur, a memory of long ago and a boat on the sea. Something inside him was beginning to unfold its wings. In his heart, the Angel of Kingship was waking up.

"*Take the sword into the church,*" said Merlin.

"*What shall I do then?*" said Arthur.

Merlin said: "*Do as you think fit. You are the king.*"

SO ARTHUR WENT INSIDE the church, holding the sword upright in front of his face. He walked slowly down the aisle, followed by all the other kings. At the altar he was met by the Bishop of London. Arthur handed the sword to him. The Bishop took the sword and, with great solemnity, he brought it down gently, first on this shoulder and then on the other, as Arthur knelt before him.

> "*With this sword I make you knight.*
> *Always fight for what is right.*
> *All the bad things hack and hew*
> *And to thyself be true.*
>
> *When the country is in your hand,*
> *When the sun hits the old stone ring,*
> *When you are married to the land,*
> *Then will you be king.*"

"*Arise, Sir Arthur!*" said the Bishop, giving the new king back his mighty and resplendent sword. Everything was very still in the church. Then, with marvellous grace, Arthur stood, raised up the sword and placed it on the altar.

"*This is the Sword of Sovereignty,*" he said in a voice which filled the church. "*It is the mark of my kingship. It must never be used against another. Let it rest with God throughout my reign!"*

So saying, he turned and came back up the aisle, leaving the sword behind him.

Well, as you might imagine, some of the greedy kings looked at the golden sword which sparkled with jewels and thought that they would rather like it for themselves.

"Oh no you don't," thought Merlin, who was watching the proceedings from the shadows of the aisle. *"You're not having that sword."* And so he covered the sword with his special Merlin-mist so that no-one could see it any more.

"Well, that's how it is," said Sir Bedivere to the boy. "Things come and things go, but just because you cannot see something does not mean it is not there."

Gwinhavar

"WHY IS IT that you are always alone?" said Sir Bedivere to the boy. "Have you no friends?"

The boy shook his head.

"But why is that?" asked Sir Bedivere kindly. "You seem a very nice boy to me."

"It's because I've got a runny nose," said the boy. "And because . . . Because I have a brother."

"Why, lots of people have brothers!" said Sir Bedivere.

"Not like mine," said the boy. "He scares everyone stiff."

"Well let's forget about brothers, shall we?" said Sir Bedivere. "And noses, too. Let's get back to our story."

WHILE WE WERE DISCOVERING Arthur to be the new Pendragon, our enemy, the Scots and Irish camped outside had fallen mysteriously asleep. Now they were waking up, and Arthur's first task as king was to win the battle of St Albans.

Although some of the Albion kings did not like the idea of Arthur being the Pendragon, things were too dangerous for squabbling, so everyone pulled together and rode out of the town to meet the enemy.

Arthur rode at our head like the king that he now was, majestic and fearless. Once the battle lines were drawn, and he gave the order to charge, he was the first into the fray. He felled everyone he met with one strike of his sword. His power seemed divine. WHOOSH! went the sword through the air. CLANG! — CRASH! — the enemy hit the ground.

And do you know, every time that Arthur raised his sword, he called on God to save the soul of his enemy.

No-one had ever seen anything like it. Suddenly the Albions were roaring with battle-lust and charging into the enemy, certain of victory. It wasn't very long before the Scots and Irish began to think that they would rather be at home.

AFTER THE BATTLE of St Albans, Arthur was not content until all Britain had been put to rights. So he made us march to Northumberland and free it from the Welsh, and then to Wales to get the Scots out. Then, just as we thought that all was well in the land, we had news that pirates from abroad had invaded Cornwall!

Cador, the King of Cornwall, who had been on campaign with Arthur, was very upset by the news. We had been thinking it was past time for Arthur to be crowned but now Arthur put aside all personal thoughts of coronation and mustered his troops. We were to go to Cornwall at once, without delay.

As we got near the castle of King Cador, our advance scouts brought news of a great siege.

Now, although still very young, Arthur had become known by his men as very cunning and a great artist in the Art of War.

"Get off your horses," he whispered down the ranks of knights, *"and do exactly as I say."*

We took soft padding from our saddlebags and, following Arthur's lead, we all tied soft-padded shoes on to our horses. What a sight! An army of horses and knights in slippers!

But Arthur hadn't finished there. We wrapped ourselves in

black sheeting, like big bed-spreads. Crouching down on our horses, we slippered forward slowly towards the castle. Slowly. Slowly. Swish. Swish. A whole army on the move, unseen, and only the softest rustle of leaves to be heard by the sharpest of ears.

"The enemy will be half-asleep and not expecting us," said Arthur. *"We'll get as close as we can before breaking cover. Follow my lead,"* he told us. None of us wanted to do anything else.

"Now!" shouted Arthur, and before the pirates could rub the sleep out of their eyes, there we were, right in the middle of them, a whole army of knights on horses with slippers on their feet, swirling swords and shouting for the enemy to surrender.

"Have mercy on us! Have mercy on us!" cried the pirates, shivering like cowards in the stern face of King Arthur.

Magnanimity is a quality of a true knight, and Arthur granted their wish for mercy, although many of us wondered why he kept doing this sort of thing to people who didn't deserve it. Having had their lives spared, the pirates returned quietly to their own lands.

NOW KING CADOR had a beautiful daughter and he had been scared that something might have happened to her. But all was well and she came out to greet her father.

She had long, curling hair as soft as moss and the colour of conkers. She had eyes the colour of bluebells. Her skin was as pale and as smooth as mushrooms and her dress was sprigged with the flowers of the woods. Well, there we were, a band of knights fresh from battle, all covered in mud and blood and pretty well stinking. The sight of this girl had a terrible effect on us. All our bravery and fearlessness left by the nearest door. Good, stout knights became shy and started to snigger like young boys.

Everyone suddenly wanted to have a bath. All the taps in the castle started to run, and throughout the place was the sound of knights singing as they scrubbed themselves clean with loofahs. When they came down to the hall at supper time, they were all pink and shining.

"The name of this beautiful princess" said Sir Bedivere, "was Guinevere. That's how you say it now in English, but in ancient British it's a lovely name — Gwin-ha-var. Go on, try it . . ."

The boy tried to say it. GWIN-HA-VAR.

"Breathe through that *H*. GWIN-HA-VAR. There, lovely isn't it? Now, where were we?"

THERE WAS A MARVELLOUS PARTY that night with music from minstrels and stories from poets. All the knights were on their best behaviour because of Gwinhavar. But we could all see that Gwinhavar only had eyes for one of us.

Arthur sat at the head of the table and, though he did not have a crown yet, he was without doubt the king of kings. As Gwinhavar twirled in the dancing, he watched her. Whenever their eyes met, the air in the hall seemed to crackle with fire.

The next day we all got up early. Our minds turned back to the prospect of Arthur's coronation. *"Now,"* we thought, *"we can crown Arthur as the rightful king of All Britain and put these battles behind us."*

But we were wrong. An arrogant messenger arrived from far-off Rome. He bore a demand that all the people of the

islands of Britain should start paying tax to the Romans. The
wretched Romans wanted to get rich without having to do
any work.

"Certainly not!" thundered Arthur in the face of the
messenger. *"Hasten back and tell your masters to pay their own
tax. You're not having ours!"*

"This will mean war!" said the messenger. Arthur accepted
the challenge.

Arthur sent word out to all the kings of Britain to raise
their armies and to gather at the channel to set forth across
the seas for France.

This was the first time that all the kingdoms of Britain had
acted together under one king. The sight brought a lump to
my throat. Thousands of men, knights and horses, under all
the flags and banners of all the British nations: Cornwall,
Scotland, Northumberland, Ireland, Wales — and all the
Middle Bits — all moving together with a single purpose.
The pounding of the drums matched the beating of our
hearts. In one short year we had changed from a group of
petty kingdoms to one great nation — and all through the
love of a king.

THE JOURNEY SOUTH THROUGH FRANCE started
very well and we soon got a rhythm in our riding. Suddenly,
however, Arthur brought us to a halt, his nose raised as if he
could sniff danger in the air. We had come to some
mountains and were about to enter a pass. But Arthur could
see that it narrowed so much that only one rider could get
through at a time.

"Go and see what is on the other side of the mountain," Arthur

commanded a young knight. He obeyed immediately, filling with pride that he had been chosen by his king for this special task. The knight squeezed his legs hard on the side of his horse to get through the gap and disappeared. We waited and waited.

At last, Arthur sent another knight. But he didn't come back either.

Arthur turned to me. *"Sir Bedivere,"* he said, *"you speak French. You go and find out what is happening. We are all relying on you."*

Well, that gap was small, and I'm a big man. I scraped the shine off my armour getting through that gap, which was damp and dark and as smelly as anything I had ever met anywhere. It went on and on. As I couldn't turn back, I had to go forward. Then, after what seemed to be an eternity, I saw a shaft of sunlight. My heart beat so loudly that the sound echoed inside my armour and then off the walls of the mountain. Whatever — whoever — was waiting for me could certainly hear me coming. But who or what would it be?

Finally I came out of this coffin-like corridor, and what an extraordinary sight lay before me! There, down in a valley, was a glistening lake, shimmering like a mirror, and in the middle of the lake was an enormous castle with a thousand pointed turrets. Its beauty took my breath away and I quite forgot my danger.

"To the grave you go, brave knight!" boomed a voice, from a place I knew not where. I spun around, shaken from my dreams.

There, standing resplendent in silver armour, was a tall knight, strong and menacing.

"Anyone who wants to go south has to get past me first. There

lie your friends," he said, pointing to a plot of freshly dug graves. *"Yours is ready and waiting for you."*

"It could be yours, of course," I retorted, for I was a knight of King Arthur. *"Let me see who you are."*

The knight lifted the front part of his helmet. To my surprise, his face was calm and his eyes were soft and kind. He did not look like someone who had just beheaded two fine knights for no good reason, but he most definitely had.

He smiled briefly and then, in a flash, his sword was drawn. I had just enough time to take my own sword up to defend myself.

"Die for your beliefs!" he cried, and his sword powered down on to mine with a crash so thunderous that I fell straight from my horse. The next thing I knew I was lying on my back and had no breath in me. The silvery knight stood over me with his sword raised. I wanted to shout: *"What about mercy? Give me mercy!"* but I had no breath. I thought, *"This is it, then — a grave for me."* And I called to God in my heart.

"Oh," said Sir Bedivere, putting his hand on his chest. "It makes my heart go pitter-pat just to think about it."

"So what happened next?" the little boy demanded.

"I'll tell you tomorrow," said Sir Bedivere.

The coronation at Carleon

THE LITTLE BOY raced to the meadow, blowing his nose hard on his handkerchief, and plumped himself down next to Sir Bedivere to hear what happened next with the silvery knight.

THERE I WAS, flat on my back and ready for death. But at that moment the sound of a charging horse filled the mountainside. *"Stop! In the name of honour for all knights!"* bellowed Arthur. He had followed me through the mountain and was now face-to-face with the silver knight. *"Fight me for your honour!"*

Arthur and the knight clashed and swung, dodged and weaved. Each time their swords met, shafts of fire spurted into the air. The noise was thunderous, ringing over the lake.

I propped myself up on my elbows out of harm's way and enjoyed a grandstand view of the fight of all fights.

"Come on Arthur!" I said to myself.

But Arthur began to tire. Just as I was beginning to wonder what might happen if Arthur lost, the silvery knight threw down his sword. *"Enough!"* he said. *"I've waited all my life to find my equal. I am Sir Lancelot of the Lake. Pray tell me Sir, who are you, for your power is sovereign and your strength divine."*

Arthur took off his helmet. *"I am Arthur, King of Britain,"* he replied, *"and no finer knight have I met than yourself. Come and join me. I will make you chief among my knights."*

At once Lancelot knelt before the king and pledged his loyalty. *"I will gladly join you,"* he said.

"What about your castle in the lake?" asked King Arthur.

"There are plenty of castles in the world," Lancelot replied, *"but there is only one King Arthur."* So saying, he left his home and never thought about it again.

Somehow we got our army through the mountain pass, though the fatter ones had to be pushed, and one was so fat that he had to be left behind. The rest of us passed on southwards to meet the Romans. They were no match for us, for now we had both King Arthur and Sir Lancelot. We won the battle on the first day, and never heard any more from the Romans about paying them tax.

MERLIN WAS WAITING for us when we got home and he told Arthur that it was time for the coronation.

"But before you are crowned," said Merlin, *"you need a wife. Who will it be?"*

Arthur blushed. *"My mind,"* he said, *"has been rather taken by the King of Cornwall's daughter, Gwinhavar."*

"What about your heart?" asked Merlin.

"That too," said Arthur, turning the colour of cherries.

So that was that. Arthur married Gwinhavar. Who, I might add, loved King Arthur dearly. At the wedding she wore a green dress made of silk with daisies embroidered on it and she had apple blossom in her hair. Merlin married them in the woods, where the trees were as tall as a cathedral.

For a wedding present, Gwinhavar's father gave the happy couple a table. It was no ordinary table. It was round and so huge that one hundred knights could sit at it.

Arthur was absolutely thrilled. It was just what he wanted.

Now he could sit down with his best friends and no-one would feel more important than anyone else, for at a round table everyone is equal.

When I say equal, I mean equally special. I can tell you, every knight in the country wanted to sit at that table, but there was only space for one hundred.

Now one of the seats at the table was a terrible thing. We called it the Seat of Shocks. Every time a new knight presented himself at court and said he wanted to join the Round Table, he was made to sit in the Seat of Shocks. But as soon as he tried to sit down the seat exploded, or seemed to. Nothing really happened but the poor knight who tried to sit on it suffered an awful feeling in his bottom as if a bomb had gone off under him.

The Seat of Shocks, Merlin told us, was reserved for someone very special indeed, but he did not tell us who this might be.

Anyway, I'm getting ahead of my story here, because all this happened much later, after Arthur had built a castle to house the table. Meanwhile he was going to Carleon in Wales with his new wife, Gwinhavar, and they were to be crowned king and queen.

NOW I DON'T KNOW if you've ever been to a coronation, but it is one of those events where everything has to be PERFECT. And I mean EVERYTHING. Palaces and churches were dusted and polished from the tops of their spires to the floors of their cellars. All knights had to polish their armour, and it is really hard to get a shine on soft metal. We were polishing and buffing for days.

But at last the hour arrived when, spick and span, we

processed through the city towards the church. Leading the procession were all the kings of Britain carrying golden swords. Sir Kay, myself, and a handsome knight called Sir Gawain followed, accompanying the King.

The Queen was accompanied by Sir Lancelot and followed by all the queens of Britain. Doves and butterflies flew about their heads. One of those queens, I should tell you, is someone who we've already met. Do you remember Morgana, the girl who had been really annoyed not to have been made the new Pendragon? Well, while we were away in France, she had grown up and had married the King of Gore. She seemed much nicer now, and had been made the lady-in-waiting of Gwinhavar.

In the church, the sacred moment finally arrived. The Archbishop of York picked up the golden crown. The whole place was in a hush. You couldn't even hear the chink of a knight's spur. To the silent echo of the witnessing angels, the Archbishop placed the crown delicately on the king's head, and then picked up that magnificent sword which Arthur had plucked from the stone.

> *"With this sword I make you king,*
> *So take it in your hand.*
> *For all time your fame will ring,*
> *And great will be the land!"*

King Arthur knelt before the altar and raised the sword aloft. A beam of sunlight caught the sword and it flashed radiantly as he placed it carefully on the altar.

AFTER THE CEREMONY, we went to the palace for the

most enormous feast you have ever seen. Arthur thought of Kay and I as his brothers, so he had given us special duties. Me he made the Royal Cup-Bearer, and Kay the Steward of the Royal Household. At the feast, therefore, Kay was in charge of seeing that all the guests were served with food, at the right time, nice and hot. To help him he had a thousand noblemen, all dressed in bright red tunics. My job was to see that each guest was served with ale. I had a thousand noblemen to assist me, and they were all dressed in blue. With two thousand guests and two thousand servants, the great hall was crowded to overflowing.

It was very hot and very noisy. Soon I felt so tired that my knees shook. But finally, after many hours, no-one could eat or drink any more. Now was the time for play.

THE KING HAD ARRANGED A TOURNAMENT, and all my strength came back as I rode out into the field with Sir Kay, looking forward to knocking a few knights off their horses. All the ladies went to the walls of the castle to watch the knights fight.

Each lady chose a knight to be her champion and to win battles on her behalf. This was the law for knights. As kings cannot be champions of ladies, Arthur asked Queen Gwinhavar who she would choose to be her champion. She looked round the knights of the Round Table thoughtfully, but then Queen Morgana whispered a little something in her ear.

"*I choose Sir Lancelot!*" said Queen Gwinhavar proudly, and King Arthur was very pleased because, by this time, Sir Lancelot had become his best friend.

Sir Lancelot knelt before the Queen and promised to be

her faithful knight and to protect her from all harm. Then he promised something else: *"I shall love the Queen as I love my own life,"* he vowed, *"and while she lives I shall never marry."*

King Arthur was very moved by Sir Lancelot's words.

All the other ladies made their choice, but fortunately no-one chose me. I didn't want to be loved by anyone, not if it makes you rattle in your armour, the way some of the other good knights were rattling while the ladies made their choices. I didn't want to dream and sigh like them.

So when the celebrations continued with a dance, I decided to slip away and be alone with the night. Just for a bit of peace and quiet.

NO-ONE WAS ABOUT. My mind was full of the wonderful day. The colours. The crowds. And of course the coronation. I found myself heading back towards the church where it all took place. Then — and you could have shaken the soreness from my bones with this — I saw someone. A woman. A very familiar woman. A woman who had an intent on her face which was certainly not for the good of anybody.

It was that Queen Morgana, again. And she had something with her which she was trying to keep hidden. No, I couldn't believe it. She had the Sword of Sovereignty and she was trying to hide it under her cloak. She had the very sword with which, just this very day, Arthur had been crowned the king of all Britain.

What were the Archbishop's words? *"With this sword I make you king, so take it in your hand..."* But now it was in the hand, not of Arthur, but of Morgana!

She seemed to sense that someone may be coming and rushed off with it under her cloak, getting the strength from who-knows-where to carry it.

Merlin should have misted it up. Why had he forgotten, I wondered?

Before I could do anything, Morgana had gone, heading towards the walls of the city that overlook the river that flows by Carleon. With a mighty strain, the queen *heeaaved* the sword up over the wall, toppling forward with the effort.

I stood there frozen in disbelief as she pushed the sword over the wall and let it go.

Down, down, down, fell the sword, turning as it went. There was a terrific splash. Water came up in a column as high as the castle walls. The heavens, awake to Morgana's act of folly, sent thunder roaring through the sky, and . . .

Sir Bedivere looked up. "I think that has to be it for today, my friend," he said, for the sky was growing as dark as his story.

The boy protested, but Sir Bedivere insisted that it was about to rain and that he should run home.

Day 6
Excalibur

THE NEXT DAY the boy found Sir Bedivere talking into the willow tree again.
"Listen," he was saying, "I can't come home for a long while yet. I'm only up
to the part about Excalibur. Will you come here? I'm feeling awfully lonely.
You will? Oh good!"

When he saw the boy, Bedivere rapped twice on the bark of the tree and
turned his back on it.

"Now where had I got to?" he asked.

The boy reminded him of the splash of the sword in the river.

YES, THE THUNDER CLAPPED, and lightning struck
the sword as it fell. Naturally I ran at once to tell someone.
Luckily the first person I met was Merlin. What I *meant* to
say to him was: *"Merlin! Queen Morgana has thrown the
Sword of Sovereignty into the river!"* But what I *did* say was:
"Is it true that gooseberry juice is made of blue cheese?"

At first he stared at me as if I was mad but then he looked
at me very gravely with his big grey eyes. *"Have you been
enchanted?"* he asked. I nodded frantically. So he said a spell
and touched my lips, and at last I found I could say what had
happened.

"Oh this is very serious," said Merlin. *"We have lost one of
the treasures of Britain! Bedivere, you are to tell no-one what you
have seen. Do you understand? I will try and put things right."*
With that, he disappeared.

ARTHUR KNEW NOTHING of what had happened. He
was in a holiday mood and decided that he would like to go

50

hunting, alone in the forest. He did not come back for days. When he did, he came on foot and he had the strangest story to tell.

He was chasing a deer for hours and hours and in the end he just gave up. Coming to a well, he got off his horse to have a drink of water. Suddenly, from out of the woods, came the most extraordinary-looking beast. It was as if you had seen all its various parts before, but never squashed into one creature. It had the feet of a deer, the body of a leopard, the bottom of a lion and the head of a snake. But the most noticeable thing was its enormous, fat, wobbly tummy which rumbled and gurgled.

Taking no notice whatsoever of Arthur, the beast snuffled away at the watering hole, burped most rudely, and then disappeared back into the woods.

No sooner had it gone than, hot and breathless, appeared the King of Wales. He was on foot.

"Have you ... (pant, pant) ... have you seen ... (pant, pant) ... the Questing Beast?" he shouted bluntly, not recognizing it was Arthur at all.

"The what?" replied Arthur.

"Don't fuss with me, man," shouted Wales. *"The Questing Beast. That bit-of-everything creature that was just here. It's killed my horse. It's my job in life to follow the beast, so I'm going to take your horse — and that's just that!"*

Arthur was astonished. Not only had he never seen such a queer beast before, but never since he had been king had anyone been so rude to him.

Without further ado, Wales jumped on Arthur's horse and rode off in pursuit of the beast with tummy troubles, leaving King Arthur to walk.

HOWEVER, LATER THAT DAY Arthur saw Wales again in the same forest. Arthur laid in wait for the horse-thief then jumped out and challenged him to a fight with swords. He fetched the King of Wales such a stunning blow that both swords broke in two. The King of Wales threw himself on Arthur and — quite against the rules — started to strangle him.

Suddenly Merlin appeared and said: *"Hold off! If you kill that man you will ruin Britain!"*

"Why?" said the King of Wales. *"Who is he?"*

"He is Arthur Pendragon."

"Oh Lord!" said Wales. Then he returned to strangling Arthur with greater effort. *"If he lives, he will kill me!"* he puffed, banging Arthur's head against the ground.

Then Merlin uttered one of his words of power and everything went still. The birds on the branches froze in mid-song, the leaves paused in their shivering, and the King of Wales fell over sideways in a great sleep. He snored deeply while the rest of the world came back to life. Merlin pulled Arthur out from underneath him.

"Why did you do that?" said Arthur angrily. *"I could have managed."*

"Of course you could," said Merlin, and took him away.

"Leave me!" said Arthur. *"I want to kill Wales when he wakes up."*

"He is the father of the knight destined to sit in the Seat of Shocks," said Merlin. *"So I suggest that you leave him alive. Come away now. We need to get you a new sword."*

HE TOOK ARTHUR TOWARDS AVALON where there was a vast lake with tall reeds on the shore. In the misty distance was an island which looked like it was floating. You could hardly tell which was land, which was sky and which was lake. As Arthur gazed across the lake, a little boat came towards them. In it was a lady; a lady who would have been most beautiful except that she was wet and had pond weed in her hair.

"Here comes the Lady of the Lake," said Merlin.

"Does she live underwater?" asked Arthur.

"Beneath the lake is a cave which leads to another world. She lives there," said Merlin.

"Another world?" asked Arthur. *"What sort of other world?"*

"Ah..." said Merlin, stroking his beard. *"It's where the gods live, and the spirits of the air, fire, earth and water. It's where things happen before they happen here. Don't you remember? You were there once..."*

For a moment, Arthur had a memory of a warm and happy place, and the shock of being plucked from it and being put on a boat ... a boat like this one now coming to the shore. He went to speak of what he remembered, but Merlin raised his hand to silence him.

The boat nestled into the reeds and the lady stepped on to the land. Merlin raised his arms in greeting. She went to speak but all she could say was *Pleugh!* and as she said it a little fish flew flapping out of her mouth. *"Ah, that's better,"* she said. *"I'm sorry — I wasn't expecting you so soon. Now,"* she said, clearing the water out of her ears with a bulrush, *"what can I do for you?"*

Merlin turned to Arthur. *"Excuse me, Sire,"* he said, *"I need to have a few words in private with the Lady of the Lake."* So saying, he led her aside and they whispered together.

Then they knelt down and started to pray, in a strange language which Merlin used when he was up to something magical.

Arthur began to feel strangely sleepy. He stretched his face, shook his head, pushed up his eyelids with his fingers: he did everything he could to stay awake. It felt as if lead weights were hanging off his eyelashes. He could hear Merlin and the Lady of the Lake but their speech was all drawn out and mumbled. Then in the lake he saw a very strange thing. He tried to focus but he couldn't. *"What is this strange . . . happening?"* he wondered blearily.

For out of the water came an arm, the white arm of a magnificent lady, and steadfastly it held aloft a sword — his

Sword of Sovereignty. Its jewels lit up the air like fireworks. Then his eyelids closed.

"Wake up, Sire! Wake up!" said Merlin.

Arthur sprang awake. All the weight had gone from his eyes and his mind had cleared. *"I thought I saw an arm in the lake,"* said he, *"holding a sword. A sword which looked like . . ."*

"You were asleep. Perhaps you were dreaming," said Merlin, before Arthur could finish his sentence. *"Here is your new sword."*

Arthur looked at the sword. This one certainly did not look like the Sword of Sovereignty. It had no jewels. It was a good, working sword, the kind of sword with which to hack and hew enemies. But he was still troubled by what he had seen.

"Merlin," he said sternly, speaking as a king rather than as a friend. *"I definitely saw my Sword of Sovereignty in the water."*

Now Merlin could not lie to King Arthur, so he told him of the treachery of Morgana, and how the sword was lost.

Arthur was very upset. *"Has she destroyed the power of my reign? — for surely that power rested in the sword I plucked from the stone."*

"The sword was saved and taken into the Otherworld," said Merlin. *"Now the Goddess has presented you with this one — a sword which may be used against your enemies. For enemies you have Sire, I'm sorry to say."*

"I shall banish Morgana!" said Arthur.

"It would be best not to, Sire. It would be best to have Morgana where you can keep an eye on her."

Arthur agreed and weighed the sword in his hand. *"It's certainly a fine weapon,"* he said. *"Quite the best I've ever handled."*

"All the best swords have names," said Merlin. *"This one is called Excalibur."*

"It has writing on it," said Arthur. *"Look, here it says 'Take me,' and here on the other side it says, 'Cast me away.' What does that mean, Merlin?"*

"It means what it says. It means, take it now, but don't throw it away until you have to. Never forget that."

"But when will that be?" asked Arthur.

"When you have no more use of it," said Merlin.

AS THEY LEFT AVALON, Arthur said: *"Merlin, this is a lovely place."*

"It is, in my opinion, Sire," said Merlin, *"one of the finest places in your entire realm."*

"I've been thinking," said Arthur. *"I need to build a hall to house the Round Table, and a castle to house the hall, and a city to house the castle."*

"Indeed you do," said Merlin.

"Somewhere near here would be lovely," said Arthur. So Merlin cut a forked twig from a tree. Holding two ends of it, he walked about the countryside with the tip of the twig held out in front of him. It pointed towards a hill. When they got to top of the hill, the twig began to jump about in Merlin's hands. Arthur looked about and saw that, in every direction, there was a wonderful view. He could even see the lake and the Isle of Avalon.

"Indeed," said Merlin, *"this is the right place."*

And as they stood on the summit of the hill, Merlin talked to Arthur about Law and Kingship.

"To rule Britain well, Sire," he said, *"you must make laws which are fair and good for the people. And to set a good*

example, you and your knights must live under four special laws."

"What are they?" asked Arthur.

"The first is — NEVER TELL LIES. The second is — ALWAYS GIVE MERCY. The third is — HONOUR THE LADIES. And the fourth is — THE KING MUST STAY AT HOME."

"Three of these laws I have always followed," said Arthur, *"but I do not understand the fourth."*

"It is for you to discover its meaning," said Merlin, and he would say no more.

The little boy was just about to ask Sir Bedivere what the fourth law meant when a small black and white cat bounded towards them, as if from nowhere.

"Oh look!" Sir Bedivere cried happily. "Here comes my wife!"

The two dragons

SIR BEDIVERE, HIS CAT AND THE BOY went for a walk. They came to some allotments, rank with weeds and neglected. Next to the allotments was a gate with a skull and crossbones on it and a notice saying "Keep Out!"

"This is poisoned land," said the boy. "They dump things here from the factory. We mustn't go inside."

Sir Bedivere looked very upset. "This is the work of the dragon," he said.

"What dragon?" asked the boy.

"There are two dragons," said Sir Bedivere. "They live deep in the land, under the earth. One is white and the other is red. They have fought since they were created, and sometimes the white one is winning, and sometimes the red. When you see that the land is starved and dying, it is the work of the Red Dragon. When the land is clean and full of growing things, it is the work of the White Dragon."

They returned hastily to the meadow. "About Excalibur," said the boy. "Was it the Sword of Sovereignty or not?"

"Yes, it was," said Sir Bedivere. "But to recover the Sword, and to alter its power so that it could be used, required deep and dangerous magic. It was necessary that no-one knew that it was the same sword, but of course, I knew."

IT WAS MERLIN WHO TAUGHT ME all about the force of the Red Dragon. *"It is necessary that your eyes be fully opened,"* he said, and with that he took from his gown a little bottle which had in it a water made from special, secret herbs. He dabbed the water on my eyes. When I opened them again, all around me were things I had never seen before. I could see the elves and fairies and the spirits which live in trees. I could see what makes the wind blow and the sun shine. And, of course, I could see the dragons. I was a knight, a brave knight, but the dragons terrified me. Merlin hit me across the back of the head.

"Remember who you are!" he said, sternly. *"Rise up knight! However strong your enemy is, you are stronger!"*

It took some time before I believed it and could walk about again without shaking. I never told anyone what had happened. I never told anyone that I could see the dragons.

ARTHUR HAD A CITY BUILT on his hill and called it Camelot. It was beautiful. All the buildings were white and shone in the sun. The power of the Red Dragon was at work throughout Britain, but at Camelot the White Dragon was served. In the lands of the Red Dragon, everyone thought only of themselves, but at Camelot we thought about others before thinking about ourselves and that made the White Dragon strong and powerful.

Now that Merlin's powers had opened my eyes, I could see that at the centre of the castle, on the ground floor, was a well with a fountain. The waters of the fountain were pure and lovely and they watered the earth beneath the castle. On the floor above the well was the round hall which housed the Round Table. Here the knights met and none of them knew about the well beneath, or the White Dragon.

Although they were the best knights in the world, none of them could see what I could see and they did not know that behind each one of them was a radiant being who looked after them. Human beings blunder about, you know, thinking that they look after themselves, but it's not true. If it wasn't for the guardians, we would all be knocking into each other and making a mess of everything.

"Have I got a radiant being?" asked the boy.

"Yes indeed," said Sir Bedivere. "Everybody has one."

The boy with the runny nose looked behind him, his eyes huge with wonder. "I can't see anyone," he complained.

"That does not mean he is not there," said Sir Bedivere. "Try asking him a question."

The boy looked behind himself again. "Please make my nose stop running," he said. Suddenly, and before he could get his handkerchief out, he gave an enormous sneeze. The trees round about swayed wildly.

"There," said Sir Bedivere. "Did you see it?"

"What?" said the boy.

"The horrible little imp that has been living up your nose just flew away."

The little boy laughed merrily, certain that he would never have to blow his nose again.

"Don't forget to say thank you to your guardian," said Sir Bedivere.

"Thanks," said the boy. "Thanks a lot."

"What happened to Morgana?" he asked. "Was she an evil witch?"

"No," said Sir Bedivere, "but she was a servant of the Red Dragon, and continued to plot the ruin of Arthur..."

THE RED DRAGON wanted badly to be rid of Arthur. Camelot was a powerful place and the White Dragon was beginning to get the upper hand. Excalibur was with the King. All that was necessary for the White Dragon to win was for the other two sacred treasures to be found. One was the hallows spear, the other was the hallows cup.

Merlin said that, now that Britain was at peace, it was time for the quest to begin.

"What quest?" asked the knights. *"A quest for what?"*

Merlin told them of the treasures, the hallows spear and the hallows cup.

"*What are they?*" asked Arthur.

"*The hallows spear brings the power of the White Dragon to the surface of the land. The hallows cup — well, it's for you to find out what it is. All I can tell you is its name, which is GRAIL.*"

"*Where will they be found?*" asked Arthur.

"*If I knew that,*" said Merlin, "*I'd go and get them myself.*"

"*But you know everything, Merlin,*" said Arthur.

"*No, Sire, not everything.*"

"Merlin, *I would like to go on this quest myself,*" said Arthur.

"*That is not possible, Sire,*" said Merlin. "*For the country to be well-governed, the King must stay where he is. It is for your knights to go on the quest.*"

"*And will they find these things somewhere in Britain?*" asked Arthur.

"*Sort of,*" said Merlin.

Well, what kind of answer was that? — *Sort of!* Arthur wanted to know what Merlin meant, but Merlin would not tell him. I knew, though, for I had already begun to see the Gates.

The Gates are everywhere and they lead to Elsewhere. Stand at a Gate and one minute you are in this world, the next you are in the Otherworld. I could see the Gates, in the forest and by the lake, in the hills and by the rivers. So I wanted to go on the quest, because I had a jolly good idea that the treasures might be found in the Otherworld.

"*Oh no, not you,*" said Merlin. "*You must stay always with the King. It is your duty as Cup-bearer. Kay must also stay.*"

A special meeting of the Round Table was held and the

Knights were told about the quest. They were all very puzzled and did not know what to make of it all, but Gawain suddenly stood up and announced that he would go on the quest. All the ladies of the court moaned and groaned. Gawain was their favourite knight and they wanted him to stay. But Gawain had a faraway look in his eyes and said that he must go. Others said that they too would go.

Arthur was very sad that so many were going on the quest. He knew, somewhere deep in his heart where you can know such things, that this was the last time he would see all his Knights of the Round Table together.

"Very well," he said to them. *"Go, and God be with you."*

So the Knights left Camelot and rode off in all directions, looking for they knew-not-what in they knew-not-where. They met all sorts of adventures: giants, wild animals and monsters of every description. They fought many battles and won many battles; they grew more brave and more powerful, but they could not find what they were looking for.

ONE DAY A KNIGHT called Sir Varlan came to a river where the grass was green and the meadows full of sweet flowers. There on the riverbank was a king who was fishing.

"What is it that you are looking for?" the king asked.

"I'm not sure," said Sir Varlan.

The Fisher King invited Sir Varlan to dine with him at his castle. Sir Varlan wondered where this castle might be, for he had seen no building for days. But when he looked round, there stood a castle, as if out of nowhere. The Fisher King took him in to dinner, and it was the most wonderful dinner that Sir Varlan had ever seen. The hall was filled with happy people who seemed to be waiting for him before they began to eat.

Now it is the rule that a knight should take off his sword and armour before sitting down to eat. Sir Varlan had done so without fear because the Fisher King seemed so good and kind. But once Sir Varlan had sat down, a knight walked past his table, so big, so muscly, and who had such very mean eyes, that Sir Varlan could not help but look at him.

"Who do you think you're staring at?" said the knight. He had a wart on the end of his nose and thought that it was the largest thing in the world and that no-one could see him but for the wart on his nose.

In fact Sir Varlan had been staring at the man himself, and his jerkin. For on his jerkin was emblazoned a violent red dragon.

"Come on," said the knight. *"Tell me — what are you staring at?"* With that, he gave Sir Varlan a hard push.

Sir Varlan did not like to be pushed. He jumped from his seat and went to draw his sword, but of course he was not wearing it. Then he noticed that the dragon knight still had his own sword on.

"Please! Gentlemen!" said the Fisher King at the head of the table. *"There will be no fighting in my hall."*

Sir Varlan turned to take his seat again, but the dragon knight tripped him up. Sir Varlan crashed, out of control, right into the food. He emerged, dripping, with beef stew all over his face. The dragon knight laughed and laughed. This was too much for Sir Varlan. He flew at the dragon knight. As quick as lightning, the knight drew his sword, ready to take off Sir Varlan's head. To gain some time, Sir Varlan threw a table at him, then another, then another. Soon the whole place was in uproar.

Suddenly Sir Varlan noticed that behind the king stood a spear, a very long spear made of crystal-glass. He made a lunge for it.

"No!" shouted the king. *"Do not use the spear!"*

The last thing the little boy wanted was for Sir Bedivere to stop at this point in the story, but stop is exactly what Sir Bedivere did.

"This was the hallows spear, wasn't it?" said the boy.

"Indeed," said Sir Bedivere. "And hallows things are sacred things and should never be used."

"Was it used?" asked the boy.

Sir Bedivere told him he would have to wait till the next day to find that out.

Day 8
The hallows spear

THE NEXT DAY, THE LITTLE BOY ran to the meadow, eager to know what happened with Sir Varlan and the crystal spear. Sir Bedivere began the story at once.

THE DRAGON KNIGHT with the warty nose was clambering over the tables, heading straight for Sir Varlan. Sir Varlan grabbed hold of the spear.

How heavy it was! As soon as he took hold of it, all Sir Varlan wanted to do was to put it down again. But it was this or die, so Sir Varlan turned the spear towards the knight.

"*No!*" cried the Fisher King again. "*Do not use the spear!*"

Sir Varlan heaved back the spear ready to push it forward. The dragon knight was coming! Sir Varlan thrust the spear forward with all the knightly might he could muster. A terrible scream pierced the ether.

It was the scream, Sir Varlan thought, of the dragon knight. But the dragon knight was still standing. And, far from screaming, he was smirking, a big evil grin on his face. Sir Varlan could not think what had happened, but then he saw someone twisting and groaning on the floor.

The kindly king! The Fisher King had taken the thrust of the spear. He had hurled himself in front of the spear so fast — as fast as a thought crosses the mind — and now he was skewered! The spear had gone right through him.

"*He must be dead!*" thought Sir Varlan, full of grief and full of confusion. "*Why isn't he dead?*"

For though the king writhed on the spear, in terrible pain, he could not die.

"*OH GOD!*" cried Sir Varlan, mortified. "*What have I done?*"

The earth began to rumble, move and heave. Cracks appeared in the castle walls, and then everything began to crash down.

Suddenly Sir Varlan woke up. He was by the stream again. When he looked around him, there was no castle. He thought for a happy moment that it had all just been a nightmare. But then he saw that all the lovely green grass was now brown, the meadow flowers were dead, and the trees were bare of leaves.

"*What have I done?*" he cried, sinking to the ground with his head in his hands.

"*What have you done?*" thundered a voice, echoing his. Sir Varlan turned to find Merlin beside him, holding two parts of a spear.

MERLIN HAD MANAGED TO GRASP hold of the hallows spear as the Castle of the Fisher King disappeared back to the Otherworld. The spear was broken. Merlin was terribly distressed. So was Sir Varlan. They made their way back to Camelot in stony silence.

As they moved through the countryside, they found plants wilting in the fields and fish floating dead in the streams. The Red Dragon was in the ascendancy.

Merlin knew he needed help. Even wizards need help sometimes. So he headed for Avalon where the Lady of the Lake lived. There she was, sitting in a puddle of water, just waiting. Merlin told her what had happened, and showed her the broken spear.

"*What can I do?*" he said.

The lady of the lake took hold of the two pieces of the spear. "*There is only one man who can mend this spear,*" she said, "*and you will find him at Camelot. If you are going that way, Merlin, would you mind taking my daughter Vivian with you? She needs to go to Camelot, but the roads are getting bad again and it's no longer safe for a young girl to travel alone.*"

Merlin agreed and the Lady of the Lake called to her daughter who came from where she had been among the reeds, talking to some swans. Merlin was still feeling very doleful and hardly noticed the girl but, as they travelled on, he began to brighten.

VIVIAN WAS A LIVELY GIRL and wanted to know

everything about everything. *"What's the name of this, Merlin?"* she would ask, pointing to a tree, and *"What's the purpose of this?"* she would ask, pointing to a herb. She had always lived with her mother in the lake and had never travelled before. Merlin was very pleased to display his knowledge and Vivian's questions made him forget his troubles.

There was no limit to her curiosity. Soon she began to ask questions about Merlin himself. No-one had asked him such questions before and he told her about where he was born and about his life as a child, when, unlike other boys, he went to school with a lunchbox full to the brim with magical herbs and potions. Vivian wanted to know all about the magic and Merlin told her everything he knew about plants such as henbane, mandrake and ragwort.

SIR VARLAN, FEELING RATHER LEFT OUT, rode on ahead and got to Camelot before them.

He threw himself at Arthur's feet.

"Forgive me, my lord, forgive me!" begged Sir Varlan. *"By a dreadful mistake I have stabbed the Fisher King with the hallows spear. The spear is now broken, and I know this is a dreadful thing because the country is turning to wasteland."*

Arthur was angry. He could feel the anger rising in him like a raging fire. *"Take this man away,"* he barked to Sir Kay. *"Take him away! I am too angry to deal with him."*

"What shall I do with him?" asked Sir Kay. There was a very good dungeon at Camelot which had never been used. Sir Kay rather hoped that here was an opportunity to throw someone in it.

"Give him breakfast and put him to bed," said King Arthur. *"He looks tired."*

"Give him breakfast and put him to bed!" grumbled Sir Kay, incredulously, as he led Sir Varlan away. *"You've brought ruin upon Britain and I am to give you breakfast and put you to bed! I suppose you want the best linen sheets?"*

Sir Varlan shook his head. *"I have made my king angry,"* he said, choking with sadness. *"I would rather have a bed of straw than linen sheets. Please starve me, Kay, and throw me in the dungeon."*

But Kay did as Arthur had ordered, gave Sir Varlan toast and jam and had a bed made for him with the best linen sheets. Sir Varlan was so upset that he could not swallow the toast. When he went to bed, he started to cry and inside himself he heard a sharp *crack!* He went into a deep sleep, so deep and so full of grief that he never woke up again.

"Sire," said Kay to King Arthur a few hours later, *"Sir Varlan is dead! He has died of a broken heart."*

NOW ARTHUR WAS FULL OF SORROW. He went to the Round Table. It was empty. He thought of his men and wondered where they all were. On each festival day, Easter, Whitsun, Pentecost, Midsummer's Day and All Hallows, knights would return to Camelot and tell of their adventures. But he knew that the Round Table would never meet all together again.

Queen Gwinhavar came and put her arm through her husband's.

"You don't look well, my lord," she said. *"You look pale."*

"I have a pain in the middle of me," he said. But he brightened a little in his wife's company and kissed her on the cheek. *"What would I do without you?"* he asked.

Just then, Merlin arrived at the castle. He arrived alone

with the broken spear. He told Arthur that it could, and at all costs must, be mended.

"Sir Bedivere," called Arthur. *"Take this spear to the workshops and make sure it is mended. I have relied on you before, and I am relying on you again now."*

Well, I tell you, the spear was incredibly heavy. There was much blood on it. I tried to clean it but the blood seemed to have sunk into the crystal and would not come out. So then I tried to mend it with glue. But, no matter what I did, the two pieces just would not stick together.

While I worked with the spear, I began to feel strange and sick. The air in the room grew hot and pressed in on me. Then, in the crystal, I started to see things. I could see the lands of Britain ruined by plagues and famine.

Then I saw something moving, something which brought back all the terror. There, moving through the spear like smoke was — the Red Dragon.

I dropped the spear with a yell and nothing would make me pick it up again.

Kay heard my scream and ran to fetch Merlin. When Merlin came, Arthur came with him. They found me, so they said later, curled up on the floor, my bones rattling with fright.

Merlin gave me one of his potions to drink which made me feel better. As I came round, Arthur was bending over me. His face was full of concern.

"What happened?" he asked.

"The spear..." I gibbered.

Arthur picked up the haft of it. Then he picked up the point. The air around us crackled and suddenly the two halves of the spear sprang together and joined into one whole again. Arthur jumped in surprise. With the spear whole, the air in the room lightened and became fresh. I got up and peered into the spear. The pictures within showed green fields and running streams.

Merlin stood with his arms raised. *"All praise to the Goddess!"* he cried. *"We are well again."*

But Arthur was not well. He never said anything or complained but sometimes, when he thought no-one was looking, he would bend double over the pain in his middle.

We put the spear in a special room. After a while, the dried blood on its point grew wet and began to drip. It dripped on to the floor and never stopped dripping. Drip. Drip. Drip. The drips ran through the floor and dripped into the room below. Slowly, slowly, the drips made their way down through the castle till they came to the well at its centre, and there they ran into the earth below. And each day, Arthur grew paler.

THE NEXT FESTIVAL was midsummer's day and many of the knights returned, including Lancelot and Gawain. All the knights had stories to tell, some wonderful, some terrible. Many said that there was trouble in the north and that many bad kings and knights had been doing dreadful things to ladies. Instead of letting ladies choose knights, knights had begun to choose ladies, and to carry them off against their will.

King Arthur reminded everyone of his law.

"A knight of the Round Table will always honour his lady," he said. *"Once he has been chosen by her, he will fight for her and protect her with his life. He will never carry her off against her*

will. Let Sir Lancelot be your example. He is the champion of my queen, and he loves her as he loves me. A good knight may love without having to possess his love. To love is to serve, not to possess."

Against all fashion, the knights of the Round Table were to treat women differently, care for them and make them happy.

When Arthur stated his law, Queen Morgana felt the power of the White Dragon increase. She looked round the hall with narrowed eyes. Something was going to have to be done, she thought . . .

Sir Bedivere walked with the boy back to the allotments. There were no leaves on the trees yet and everywhere seemed dead. One or two plots had been dug over but many parts were still covered in brambles and dead thistles. "There is much work to be done here," he said. "Bring some tools with you tomorrow."

Day 9
The Wrong Thing

THE BOY ARRIVED THE NEXT DAY with a billhook which he had borrowed from his father. Sir Bedivere showed him how to cut swathes through the weeds.

"The thing about wastelands is that they spread," said Sir Bedivere. "They are catching, like the measles or 'flu. To care for the land is to call up the power of the White Dragon. Now, where were we? — Oh, yes..."

AT THE MIDSUMMER FESTIVAL we held a ball at Camelot. The ladies were all allowed to choose their partners, but no-one chose me. You see, I dance like a bear with two left feet, and everybody knows it.

The daughter of the Lady of the Lake was at the ball, and Merlin followed her everywhere with his eyes and kept muttering: *"Choose me, choose me!"* But Vivian was queuing up with the rest of the ladies for the chance to dance with Sir Gawain. I left Merlin to fret by himself and went outside on to the battlements.

It was a lovely moonlit night. Out on the battlements I found Lancelot and Gwinhavar taking the air. They looked happy enough, but not as happy as they would have looked if King Arthur had been with them. My poor lord was still very pale and had excused himself to go to bed early.

Suddenly I felt the warm breath of a woman behind my ear. My nostrils filled with a most horrid perfume. It smelt like one of Merlin's potions which had gone badly wrong. It was Queen Morgana — again.

"*You have the eyes to see,*" she whispered. "*What do you see?*"

"*I see the bravest knight in all the world and the beautiful queen of my beloved king,*" I said.

"*Oh, come, come, Bedivere,*" she hissed. "*Is that all you see? Why not look again?*"

Now, women who smell like that can cause a man to become confused. "*What else is there to see?*" I demanded sharply, pinching my nostrils.

Morgana, realising that she was not having the effect on me that she wanted, twirled angrily in front of me. "*You could see the truth — two wonderful people happy at being alone together, walking so close that their bodies can't help but touch, and all under the moonlight of love . . . If you can't see that, then you're more of a fool than I thought you were!*"

With that she twirled away, her cruel laughter drifting over the battlements and down to the valley below.

"*What a woman,*" I thought. "*She doesn't have the eyes to see, or she would know that Lancelot and Gwinhavar are missing their king, and that they are together because they both love him.*" Or perhaps she could see that, and she wanted the rest of us to see something else. Was that it?

AT THAT MOMENT I quite literally bumped into Sir Tristan of Lyonesse, who was also taking the air and gazing at the moon. I told him what had happened and how, in my opinion, the poisonous Morgana was trying to spread evil rumours.

To my horror, Tristan thought that Morgana knew more about things than I did. "*You see, my friend,*" he said. "*Love works like that. But you wouldn't know anything about love,*"

would you Bedivere? It's you, my good fool, whose sight is deluded, not Morgana."

Now that was the second time in as many moments that I had been called a fool. A fellow can start to doubt himself if he gets told something often enough.

"What do you mean, Sir Tristan?" I demanded.

Sir Tristan then began to tell me his awfully sad story, of how he had been sent to Ireland to bring back the Princess Isolda as a wife for the King of Cornwall. On the way he had fallen in love with Isolda, and she with him. But he had done his duty and, against every urge in his heart, had given her to the King of Cornwall. He stood looking at the moon with tears in his eyes.

"And I know," he said, *"that in Cornwall she is looking at the same moon through the same tears."*

Whatever was happening to the Knights of the Round Table? The whole of Camelot seemed to be under the spell of the moon and love. There was only one solution to this midsummer madness — I would go and talk to the owls in the wood, and perhaps have a jolly good fight with a ghost.

IN THE WOOD the owls and all the other beasts didn't want to talk so I sat down to ponder on the meaning of life and grew drowsy. Then, just as I was dropping off, I became aware of something breathing. Something very large. Breathing very hard. It was sort of whistling and moaning in its sleep.

Dawn was coming and my eyes could just begin to discern the shape of a beast, the queerest beast I had ever seen. It had a great fat tummy which rumbled whilst it slept. It seemed very troubled and sometimes twitched violently as if dreaming of something terrible.

Then, as if out of the dawning light itself, sprang a knight on horseback with sword lifted, all puffed up and ready to slaughter the sleeping beast with one foul stroke.

I just got my wits back in time.

"*Stop!*" I shouted at the lunging knight, for I could see no good reason to kill a beast while it slept. As I shouted, the queer beast woke up with a piercing scream. Then it burped. No ordinary burp, mind you. But a burp the blast of which fair knocked me off my feet. The beast crashed off through the woods and was gone.

"*How dare you spoil my life's work?*" shouted the knight. "*I am the King of Wales, no less, and I have been trying to get that beast for years and years. You will lose your head for this!*"

He lifted his sword, and as it flashed in the first morning sun, and as my thoughts were turning towards heaven, we both heard the cry of a girl's voice from somewhere deep in the woods.

"*That soulds like a damsel in distress,*" I said, appealing to the king's knightly honour. For, although he had little regard for most rules, he was still a knight of Round Table, and even he could not ignore a damsel in need of rescue.

"*You've been lucky this time. But next time...*" shouted the King of Wales as he turned and galloped off towards the sound of the cry.

I couldn't quite hear what would happen to me next time.

JUST AS I WAS THINKING that Merlin was behind this somewhere, a pretty maiden appeared right in front of me. A pretty maiden — with a beard!

"Merlin," I said. *"Is there something wrong with you? Your magic does not seem to be what it was."*

"Oh, I'm alright," huffed Merlin, turning back into his own shape. But I could see that he wasn't. He seemed to have the same look on his face as Sir Tristan had when he was telling me his love story.

"Not Merlin, too," I thought to myself.

There was only one thing for it — take him out of himself by calling on his knowledge.

"Merlin," I said, *"what is the Questing Beast?"*

"It is The Wrong Thing," said Merlin.

"The King of Wales seems determined to catch it," I said.

"Well, he is chasing The Wrong Thing."

"Merlin," I said, *"I wish I could go on the quest for The Right Thing."*

"It will be enough that it is found. It does not have to be you who finds it. You must stay at Camelot and look after your king," said Merlin. With that he changed into a little deer — a deer with a beard — and ran off into the woods.

WHEN I RETURNED TO CAMELOT, Sir Tristan of Lyonesse had left a message for me to join him at breakfast. He felt sorry for having called me a fool.

"Merlin's in love," I said, hoping to impress him with at least a passing knowledge of the subject.

"Wizards don't fall in love, my good man," replied Sir Tristan. *"It only happens to people like you and me."*

"People like you, perhaps," I said. *"Not me. I'm immune from this mad disease."*

"What a lot of old toffee apples you sometimes talk, Bedivere,"

79

said Sir Tristan. *"Every man has a heart. Even you . . ."*

"I've never loved any lady, and I never will," I said hotly.

"Oh yes you will," said Sir Tristan, knowingly and with a very smug smile.

Sir Tristan left later that day for Lyonesse.

WHEN HE CAME BACK TO COURT, at the time of All Hallows, he brought with him a little black and white kitten. *"This is for Sir Bedivere,"* he said, presenting it at the Round Table. *"He needs to have someone to love."*

The little kitten was called Megan. I did not know quite what to do with her. I was sure that all the knights of the Round Table wanted to laugh at me, but they kept their faces as straight as spears.

"I've never heard of a knight with a kitten," I said. *"I shall give her to the queen."*

"That would offend me and I would be your enemy for ever," said Sir Tristan. I think he meant it. So I picked up the kitten and took her back to where I slept in the barracks.

"You sleep there," I said sternly to the kitten, and put her in one of my boots. But as soon as I was settled, she climbed out of the boot and on to my bed. Then she walked the length of me and, coming to the crook of my arm, she snuggled down and gave a tiny little sigh. It was a little puff of contentment. I had never been loved by anyone before. Nor had anyone ever seen the crook of my arm as somewhere to shelter. The next thing I knew, a little sigh came out of me too. So we snuggled down together for the night, nose to nose, and breathed the same air as we slept. After that, Megan and me, we went everywhere together.

Now the knights of the Round Table all wore crests on

their helmets, each one different from the rest. One of the
first things that Megan did when she came into my life was
to chew up the three feathers that I wore as a crest. Then she
took to sitting on my head in their place. So my crest became
a cat, a real cat when I was at home, and a cat moulded in
soft metal when I was in battle.

As he came to the end of his tale, the little black and white cat bounded up
Sir Bedivere's back and sat on his head and held her nose up proudly to the
wind.

"When did she become your wife?" asked the boy.

"Later," said Sir Bedivere. "At the end of the story."

Day 10
Merlin and Vivian

THE NEXT DAY the knight and the boy returned to work on the allotments. Their efforts encouraged and inspired those who owned the plots, and they also came to do some work. Eventually Sir Bedivere led the boy away.

"I think we can leave them to it, now," he said. They went to the riverbank where Sir Bedivere sat down to continue the tale.

THE QUEST FOR THE GRAIL wasn't proving easy. In fact the questing knights were having a thunderous lack of success. They were getting confused and could not remember what they were looking for, or why.

"*Why don't we try to remember what we know about the Grail so far,*" I suggested one evening over our mugs of ale.

"*Bedivere,*" said Sir Tristan, mockingly, "*that is one of your more intelligent suggestions. See what a good cat can do for a man!*"

In life you get used to sniping comments, so I just ignored him.

"*Now we all know that there are three treasures of Britain, the hallows sword, the hallows spear and the hallows cup,*" I said. "*The Sword of Sovereignty we have.*" As no-one knew that we had lost it, or that it was now with us again in the form of Excalibur, I passed quickly on. "*And we know that the hallows spear was found and broken, and our beloved king put it back together again. And we know that Sir Varlan died of a broken heart...*"

Suddenly a bolt of mental lightning flashed in my mind.

"*And we know,*" I said, very hesitantly, "*that ever since the hallows spear has been put . . . together . . .*"

"*Yes, go on, don't stop!*" urged the other knights.

"*Since it has been put together, BLOOD has not stopped dripping from its tip . . .*"

"*Yes, go on, go on . . .*"

"*And our beloved King Arthur has looked paler, and paler, and paler.*"

"*That is just coincidence,*" said Sir Tristan, captivated by the story.

"*What may be a coincidence in this world is not in the Otherworld,*" I said with conviction. "*I have a strong hunch that nothing will go right until we find the hallows cup.*"

"*But what is this Grail?*" asked one weary knight.

"*Yes, what is it? What exactly are we looking for?*" shouted another of my brothers-in-arms.

"*We need Merlin,*" I said.

We all fell silent. We waited. As Merlin hears all conversations with his magical ears we thought he would turn up soon. But we had to wait a long time. A very long time. In fact, it took him two whole weeks to turn up, which for him is a very, very long time indeed.

"*I'M SORRY to have kept you waiting,*" said Merlin.

"*Bedivere must be right,*" said King Arthur, looking fondly towards his wizard. "*You have fallen in love, Merlin.*"

"*No, no,*" said Merlin. "*It's not love. Not at all. It's folly. We all have the seeds of folly in our hearts, but I thought mine had died by the fire of wisdom. Now, under the sunshine of a young maid's smile, BOOM! Folly-weeds everywhere. They've choked my magic. Folly-weeds and passion flowers . . .*"

So these days I can't just appear. I have to walk."

Merlin drifted off into melancholy thought for a moment, then said, *"What is it you want to know?"*

"The Grail, Merlin. What is it, and what does it look like?"

> *"All I can say is that It sees all things, but cannot Itself be seen; It hears all things, but cannot Itself be heard; It lives nowhere but is everywhere at the same time. It flows inside the cup, but is forever outside it."*

With that Merlin stopped, looking most forlorn.

The knights were stunned to silence. Merlin's mysterious words had made the Grail more alluring, and at the same time even more difficult to picture.

Merlin suddenly swung round to King Arthur.

"Please Sire, you must lock me up in a sanctuary so that my folly is starved of light and is slain. Then I can get back to my normal self," he said.

King Arthur obeyed, reluctantly, and put Merlin in a chapel with a very secure bolt and key. He listened at the keyhole and heard Merlin sigh and say a name over and over: *Vivian ... Vivian ... Vivian ...* So it was the daughter of the Lady of the Lake who had enchanted his wizard!

Merlin really had wanted to be locked up and cured but, as soon as we left him, the folly-weeds and passion flowers got the better of him. *"Oh dear, I can't stay here,"* he muttered and, turning himself into a shadow, he slipped out through a gap under the door.

The next day, when we took food to the wizard, we found the chapel still locked but empty.

VIVIAN SAT BY THE LAKE OF AVALON combing her long wet hair. Suddenly she noticed that she had two shadows. One was hers and the other was that of an old man with a very long beard.

"Is that you, Merlin?" she said. Now Vivian did not like Merlin, but you would not think so to hear her speak. She spoke so sweetly that Merlin materialised from his shadow. He appeared beside her.

"Vivian..." he said wistfully.

"Now what secrets are you going to tell me today?" she asked with some briskness.

She already knew how to change her shape and make the rain fall when it was dry; how to see the future and make the sun come out when it was cold. Merlin had taught her practically everything he knew.

"I could show you how to make your nose click," he said.

"That's just a trick," said Vivian scornfully. *"I want real magic."*

She was getting very fed up with Merlin. She was only interested in his secrets and if he had no more...

"I could show you my cave," he said.

"Very well," sighed Vivian, rising to follow him. *"Show me."*

Merlin had never shown anyone his cave before. He led Vivian to a rocky valley. At first there was no cave to be seen, but Merlin pronounced a word, low and heavy, deep in his throat. It sounded like *AGARFIXAS*. Suddenly a great boulder trembled, rumbled and moved to one side. Behind was the entrance of a deep cavern.

"Is that the word which has power over stones?" Vivian asked.

"*Yes it is,*" said Merlin, sadly. It was his most precious secret. He went to the cave. "*Will you come in?*" he said.

"*No, I don't think so.*"

"*Oh please, Vivian, please,*" he said. "*This is my own private place. No-one in the world knows about it. Only you. Please come and see it.*"

"*Well, you go in first and make sure that there are no dragons.*"

So Merlin went in. "*Please come in Vivian, oh please. There are no dragons in my home. Please come.*"

Now it vexed Vivian to hear proud Merlin pleading and begging. Her mind filled with anger, like a burning fire. The fire in her mind created an intense heat, the heat of more than a hundred suns. Vivian gasped for air, but the air only fanned the fire.

Then out of her mouth came the magic word — a strange sound, deep and heavy, the likes of which she had never made before. *AGARFIXAS!*

All the rocks around started to move. Boulders as big as palaces shook. Cracks appeared in mountain sides, and huge boulders began to fall. One fell right across the face of the cave.

Merlin was trapped!

The mountains stopped juddering and everything became still. Vivian stood staring. She could see nothing but smooth rock where the cave had been. "*Merlin!*" she screamed, but there was no reply.

Terrified of what she had done, she turned on her heels and ran back towards home.

She ran and ran and ran. But as she ran, all the bushes in the valley closed behind her, as if she had never been there.

All the trees closed over the valley, as if the valley had never been there. She could never, ever, find Merlin's cave again. And nor could anyone else.

VIVIAN WAS NOT ALL BAD. No-one ever is, no matter how foolish they may act, or how unkind they may be. She did not have the courage to go to King Arthur and tell him what she had done, but she tried to make amends by using all the magic knowledge Merlin had given her as a force for good. She lived by a well near Camelot, where she could keep her hair nice and wet, and she took it upon herself to be kind to whoever or whatever came her way.

What came her way one day was the Questing Beast with the rumbling stomach. It dipped its head in the well to drink.

"You have a very bad tummy there," said Vivian, in the kindest voice the beast had ever heard.

It was just about to relax, to sit down and perhaps drop its tired head in the lap of the kind maid, when the King of Wales crashed out of the forest and rushed towards them.

Vivian, using one of Merlin's magic words, stopped the king in his tracks.

"Why are you chasing this beast?" she demanded.

"I want to find out what it is and how it works," said the King of Wales, rather taken aback by such a question from a mere maiden.

"And how will you do that?" Vivian enquired, again in a firm but friendly manner.

"By cutting it up and looking inside it," said the king.

"But it would die!" Vivian cried.

"Yes, but my knowledge would be all the greater for it," said the king.

"Let me give you some real knowledge, good Sir Knight," replied Vivian. *"You have not been home for twelve years. This I know. You have never seen your youngest son. This I know. All this time you've been chasing the Wrong Thing. This I know. But it is that son of yours who will find the Right Thing."*

The King of Wales was astonished. The strange maiden with wet hair and true knowledge had somehow freed his heart of its burdens. After all these years of chasing the Questing Beast, he suddenly felt like giving up and going home. Which is what he did.

As the king rode towards Wales, he laid down to rest. Into his dreams came a cup, a cup overflowing with light. Thinking thus of the Right Thing, he died peacefully in his sleep.

"What happened to Merlin?" asked the boy. "And the Questing Beast?"

"Some say that they have seen Merlin, but not as he used to be. Sometimes he's a shadow, sometimes he's like a ghost. Sometimes he's the flicker of a flame in the fire. But he's always around in times of need, around without really being there. As for the Questing Beast — set free from the desire of the King of Wales, it lived a long life, free of stress, and never burped again."

Day 11
The fool

"WHAT I WANT TO KNOW," said the boy the next day, "is what's the Right Thing?"

"Oh now that's a very good question," said Sir Bedivere. "Of all questions anyone could ask, it must be the best. It's time that I should tell you about the knight who was different from the rest."

WE HAVE TO GO BACK IN TIME twelve years to the court of the King of Wales. It was then that the King of Wales left home to join the armies of Arthur mustering to go to war with the Romans, and before he started chasing the Questing Beast.

"*Please don't go!*" cried his wife, the Queen of Wales.

She had had six sons. All had grown to be knights. All had died in battles. Knightly adventures and war caused her nothing but grief.

"*I'm about to have another child,*" she told him. "*If you go to war, you will never come back. I know it. You will never see him! He will never know his father!*" Then she really began to sob and cry.

But the king had the bugles and trumpets sounded and his resplendent Welsh army marched out of the castle and took the road to join Arthur.

A few days later, the queen gave birth to a new son. She worried for him. Then an idea struck her.

"*Of course!*" she said. "*I will become a peasant. Then my son will never know about knights, adventures and battles. Then he will grow and grow, right up into old age.*"

Her daughter, Dindrane, was only two years old, and was as happy to be a peasant as to be a princess. In the dead of night, the queen took her and the baby and left her rich castle and her rich lands to go to the forest and be blissfully poor.

Well, this act of the poor, silly queen was the best thing that had happened to the Red Dragon for some time. Since Arthur had become king, it had felt quite weak. Now it had all Wales to itself.

"*HURRAH!*" it roared as it rushed through the land. "*All Wales to myself!*" And it rushed about inspiring havoc in a land left without a strong ruler.

So twelve years passed, and a little boy called Parsifal grew up in the woods thinking that he was the son of a poor woman and the brother of a peasant girl.

WHEN THE KING OF WALES DIED, Arthur moved his court to Carleon where, many years before, he had been crowned. He wanted to keep the peace in Wales, and so every day he would send Kay and I out on patrol.

One day we were out with Sir Gawain, who had returned to court after yet another staggeringly hopeless quest for the Holy Grail. We came to a forest and rode in under the tall, leafy trees. There we came upon an old woman with a boy and a girl running happily around her. When she saw us, the old woman grew frightened and pulled the children close to protect them.

"*We mean you no harm, madam,*" said Sir Gawain.

The boy struggled free from his mother and ran up to us. You should have seen the look on his face! I have never seen such wonder. He was a simple peasant boy and he looked at us as if we were gods.

"*Come away, Parsifal!*" said the old woman.

"*Madam, we mean you no harm,*" Sir Gawain said again.

The boy walked around my horse and ran his hand over its flanks lovingly. He looked up at me. "*I want to be like you!*" he said.

"*Parsifal!*" shouted his mother. "*Come away!*"

"*What are you?*" he asked me.

"*Why, we are knights. Have you never seen a knight before?*"

"*I've lived in the forest all my life,*" said the lad. "*What are knights and what do you do?*"

"*We are warriors trained in the Art of War. We three are companions of King Arthur and keep the peace in Britain.*"

"*I want to come with you!*" cried the lad.

The poor woman was growing frantic and dragged the struggling Parsifal away. The three of us rode on. Kay and Gawain thought no more about it. But having had Merlin's potion in my eyes, I could see things which, to others, aren't really there. And what I saw in the young lad was a beam of brightness, like a shooting star in the night sky.

Now of course the old woman was the Queen of Wales, or had been. She never mentioned it to her children. Dindrane had a dim memory of a palace and a wonderful garden, but Parsifal knew nothing but the woods. He had never heard of knights before. But as soon as he had seen us, he knew that, in truth, he was one himself. The time had come for him to leave the forest and fulfil his destiny.

"*I AM GOING TO BE A KNIGHT!*" he announced to his mother. "*I must have weapons and armour and a horse.*"

"Dear God," said his mother.

"What is God, mother?" he asked, for Parsifal had never heard mention of God before.

"He is Light beyond all light, brighter than a summer's day," said his mother.

"Then I will look for that Light, and I will serve it always," said Parsifal.

Throughout his life he had liked to hunt and had made himself spears and holly darts. He now went to fetch them from the hut where he lived. His mother, knowing in herself that she could keep him no longer, saddled a bony old nag that they kept. She dressed Parsifal up in rough sacking.

"This is not armour!" said Parsifal, thinking of how the knights had glinted in the sun.

"Let simplicity be your protection," said the old lady.

Parsifal loved his mother and was very sorry to be leaving her, but a shooting-star feeling was with him. *"Mother, do you have any other advice?"* he asked.

"Indeed I do," she said. *"Stop asking questions. Keep quiet and pretend to know something even when you don't know it, lest people think you are a fool."* Parsifal repeated this advice to himself so as always to remember it.

HE RODE AS HARD AS THE NAG would allow. When he arrived at our base at Carleon, the court was the scene of a furious argument. A knight with red hair, red beard, red face and wearing white armour was frothing and foaming at the king, saying that some of his lands had been stolen and that he wanted them back. The knight stormed from the hall. He would be in the meadow, he said, ready to meet whoever came out to challenge him.

At that very moment Parsifal arrived in the hall.

"I have come here to be made a knight!" said the lad, standing proud in his sack-cloth armour and confident in his home-made spears.

I'm afraid that everyone found this sight extraordinarily funny. We laughed and laughed. Parsifal did not know what the joke was. Remembering his mother's advice, he could not ask, so he just laughed with us.

"You're too young, cub!" said King Arthur, his kind eyes gazing on the boy.

But Sir Kay stepped forward. *"Sire,"* he said. *"Why not send him out to meet the Red Knight? Then we can all get on with our dinner."*

"No!" said Sir Gawain. *"That's a cruel idea. The Red Knight will kill him!"*

"He will not!" said Parsifal, puffing up his chest. *"I am a match for any knight."*

With that he left the hall and rode out to the field where the Red Knight waited. The Red Knight was astonished to see a mere boy coming out to meet him. And, what's more, a boy dressed in sacking. He was furious.

"Go away!" he shouted. *"Send me a real knight!"*

"I'm as real as any knight!" Parsifal shouted back. With that he lined up his old pony. Something moved within him. It was that shooting-star feeling. But this time it tingled from the tips of his toes, up through his knees, into his bottom, and right up his spine. He felt at least ten feet tall. Defeat was impossible!

Something of this bright new energy even entered the bony old nag. Parsifal and the horse waited calmly as the Red Knight charged, a great heap of metal pounding across the field. Parsifal heard the echo of his mother's words in his ears: *"God is the Light beyond all light, brighter than a summer's day."*

Everything became very, very, clear. It was as if all darkness disappeared from his eyes, and the form of the charging Red Knight focused in his sight as an unmissable target. Slowly, with attention acute enough to pierce the eye of a passing sparrow, Parsifal took out one of his wooden spears and hurled it with the strength of light towards his foe.

The Red Knight toppled from his horse and crashed to the ground. The spear had passed right through the gap between his helmet and his armour.

Parsifal dismounted and approached the dying knight. He did not know that it was a rule that, at the end of any contest, a knight should be told who it was who had killed him so that his soul could go free.

"Ask me who I am!" groaned the Red Knight. *"And tell me who you are."*

"No, I will not ask," said Parsifal. *"My mother told me never to ask questions."*

At that the Red Knight heaved a tormented sigh and Parsifal saw the life flow out of the body.

BY THIS TIME we had finished our dinner, and Sir Gawain thought he would check up on the young sack-cloth peasant. Imagine his surprise and delight when he found the boy bending over the vanquished Red Knight.

"Take his armour, Parsifal. It is yours," said Sir Gawain. *"Put it on and present yourself to your King."*

So Parsifal strapped himself into his foe's armour. He felt

like a small pea in a very large pod. He clanked his way into the hall.

"He has won the contest," said Sir Gawain to King Arthur. *"You must honour him, Sire."*

King Arthur agreed. He took Excalibur and placed it now on this shoulder and now on that and declared Parsifal to be a knight of the Round Table.

Sir Kay was in a wicked mood. *"Sit with us, boy,"* he said, and led Parsifal to the Seat of Shocks. We all fell quiet, waiting for the big bang.

"Thank you, Sir," said Parsifal and sat down. There was silence. Nothing happened!

The hall filled with an excited murmuring, growing in

intensity. We all stared at the boy. No, not a boy. Now a man. A man who was not only fulfilling his own destiny but the destiny of the Round Table.

"*You will stay with us, Sir Parsifal,*" said King Arthur, the glint of a question in his voice.

But Parsifal did not want to stay in the court. He suspected that what he was looking for was not to be found there.

"*Forgive me, Sire,*" he said, "*but I think I will go on now. I am looking for the Light beyond all light, and that will I serve.*"

So saying, he left the court.

His words troubled Sir Gawain, who had been at court now for many months. "*I'd like to go and look for that Light, too,*" he said.

"Tell me, Sir Bedivere," said the boy. "The Light beyond light — the Grail — the Right Thing. Are they all the same?"

"Correct!" said Sir Bedivere, most pleased.

The court of the Fisher King

THE BOY ARRIVED EARLY on the next day, hoping that at last he might hear about the Right Thing. Sir Bedivere was happy to oblige.

WHEN PARSIFAL LEFT CAMELOT there was only one thought in his mind. The Light. The Light beyond all light. It never occurred to him how silly he looked, rattling about in the Red Knight's shining white armour.

On the road he met an old crone with a face full of warts. She seemed to come out of nowhere.

"You look dreadful," she croaked. *"Get some muscle on you, boy."*

Well, Parsifal thought that she looked pretty dreadful as well, but he was too polite to say so. Besides, she was right.

So he went to a retired knight who lived alone in the forest. The old man put him through some really tough exercises. And each night, over a sizzling camp fire, he talked to Parsifal of war-craft, weapons, and all the things knights have to know about. As months passed, so Parsifal began to fill his armour.

Then one day the old knight said: *"Your training is complete. Off with you. Go where you will."*

"Go where you will?" thought Parsifal. *"What on earth does that mean?"*

Not knowing, Parsifal just decided to go where his horse went. There really didn't seem much else he could do, and, after all, it wasn't much use him going in one direction and his horse in another.

NOW ALL THIS KNIGHTLY TRAINING came in very
handy indeed. One day, Parsifal happened upon a magnificent
castle. Its walls reached up to the heavens, and through a
little window right at the top he could see a beam of sunlight,
coming and going, like a beacon flashing a message.

Inside himself he could feel that shooting-star feeling
again. Up from his toes, up through his knees, up into
his bottom, and then right up his back. *"What is happening
to me?"* he wondered. But before he could think a huge
knight, covered with a mask of evil, challenged him
thunderously.

"I am the servant of all things wicked," roared the evil
knight. *"Get out of my way, for in the castle lies a treasure that
belongs to me and no-one else, anywhere."*

Before Parsifal knew it, that shooting-star strength was
charging down his arm and straight into his sword. The
sword flashed into the air, creating such a hurricane force
around that leaves flew off the trees. With one well-aimed
stroke, the sword dashed against the evil knight, sending him
crashing to the ground.

*"Stop! Have mercy! I surrender to you, whose power is even
mightier than my own,"* bellowed the evil knight. Parsifal,
remembering his training in knightly virtue, accepted the
surrender on condition that the knight swore allegiance to
King Arthur.

Now what was inside the castle that the evil knight
claimed to be his own, which no-one else could have?
Parsifal entered very cautiously.

*"Bravest of all warriors, welcome to my home. You have
rescued me from the wicked knight, and I shall always honour you
as my protector and lord."*

The voice came from a sight such as Parsifal had never seen before in all his life. For there stood a most radiant princess. She shone with a light, so fine and so pure, that if you held your hand in front of it, a beam would go clean through.

"*My name is Blanche,*" she said. "*Princess of the White Castle. What is it that makes you stare so, and why don't you speak?*"

"*I think I see God,*" said Parsifal, finding the words from somewhere. "*For I think I see the Light which is beyond all other lights.*"

The princess smiled. "*I am not the Light, I am only the mirror of the Light,*" she said.

Parsifal remained rooted to the spot. He really wanted to ask a question. Not just any question. THE question. "*Will you . . . ?*" he began. "*No,*" he thought. "*My mother said never to ask questions.*"

Blanche waited and waited, but the question never came. At last she said to him: "*You are my lord. You and I are married. We are husband and wife.*"

"*Oh good!*" cried Parsifal. He was mightily relieved at having got through without asking THE question. It all seemed to show that mother's advice was right. Parsifal was filled with bliss.

BLANCHE WAS A PERFECT WIFE. She seemed to know what Parsifal was thinking even before he did, which was just as well, for he never would ask a question. One day, Blanche knew that Parsifal knew that he had to move on. The Light was calling.

"Go, my brave lord," she said to him softly. *"I already am wherever you are. You are never without me. Should you need me, just call my name."*

Parsifal left the court very happily. But this time he forgot to let his horse choose the way, for he was determined to find what he was looking for, and quickly, too.

He looked, and searched, sometimes going one way, sometimes another. At last he came to a bleak marshland full of fog and there he soon became lost. His heart felt heavy, as if a dark cloud had entered into it. He bowed his head. *"Oh Blanche..."* he sighed.

As he did so, a beam of sunlight came out of the clouds and threw shadows on the ground. Three shadows. There was his own shadow. There was the shadow of his trusted horse. But there was a third shadow too.

Parsifal looked around to see who else was there, but he was all alone. He looked back at the shadows. The third was still there. The third shadow moved, and began to take the form of an old, sad man with a very long beard — its arm and its beard rose up and pointed forth the way.

Now there had been many stories in the past about Merlin the Wizard who was old and had a beard. But, as Parsifal had heard it, Merlin had disappeared many years ago and no-one could find him. *"If it isn't Merlin, then who is it?"* Parsifal thought. But he didn't dare ask the shadow who he was because mother had told him not to ask questions.

Parsifal turned his horse and followed in the direction he had been shown. His faithful horse plodded along, and Parsifal drifted into a hazy sleep.

SUDDENLY A SHOOTING STAR rocketed up into his

head and he woke up with a tremendous start. There, right in front of him, forming before his very eyes, was a castle. Parsifal entered its huge gates and came to a great hall where hundreds of courtiers were feasting at a table which went on and on and did not stop.

At the end of the hall was a bed and in the bed was a king who was very sick. It was the Fisher King, whom Sir Varlan had wounded with the hallows spear. The king could not eat but he was very happy for all his courtiers to be eating. He greeted Parsifal and invited him to dine.

"Whatever I have is yours," he said.

Parsifal shyly took his place at the tables. The food was magnificent. He had never seen such abundance. Everybody's plate was piled high with lovely things but Parsifal's plate was empty. He did not know that in the court of the Fisher King all you had to do was to think of your favourite food and it would appear on your plate.

He stared at his plate and his plate stared back at him. The plate thought: *"He's a fool, so I will give him fool's food."* The next time Parsifal looked down at his plate he found a jacket potato filled with rice pudding.

Suddenly a tiny bell rang. *Piiiiiinnng!* The sound seemed to go on forever. A sweet scent of hyacinths filled the air. At the last note of the bell, all the doors and windows closed, as if by themselves. Then the ghost of a sword appeared, a magnificent sword encrusted with jewels. After the sword, as if in a procession, came the ghost of a spear. Parsifal was amazed to see that the tip of the spear dripped blood. At the sight of the spear, a very large moan came from the king in the bed. It was, of course, the ghost of that spear which had given him his deathly wound.

103

After the spear came a maiden, dressed all in white. She held out her hands in front of her as if she were holding the most precious of crystal cups.

Parsifal looked again, his attention absolutely centred on the maiden's hands. There was no cup that he could see. It was a transparent cup, out of which light was pouring in an endless stream. It was as if the light was flowing inside the cup but was forever outside it, a Light coming from beyond all light.

Parsifal gazed at the Light and felt himself fill with it until he shone. He was speechless with awe. As the vision of the procession disappeared, the company in the hall turned to stare at Parsifal. Parsifal said nothing. He hid his head in his hands and tried to remember the Light. But when he looked up again, it was all gone: the company and the king, the feast in the hall, the castle itself. All had gone. Parsifal was back where he had started. On his horse.

HE WAS SO SAD — he had found what he had been looking for, and now he had lost it. He had failed in the quest. *"I might as well go home,"* he thought, full of despair.

Suddenly his horse snorted in fear as the loathsome old crone with warts appeared again, as if from nowhere.

"Parsifal of Wales," she said. *"You are a goose!"*

"What do you mean?" he said angrily.

"You had the Grail before your very eyes, but you did not cure the king." Her voice was as ugly as her face but, believe it or not, she meant well.

"Worse," she continued. *"You have a cold heart. You have never written to your mother or tried to find out how she is. That Red Knight that you killed — he was your uncle, and the lands*

which he fought for were your lands in Wales. All is now lost. You are stupid, the most stupid knight ever. The fate of Britain depends on the healing of the wounded Fisher King. You could have done what needs to be done. But you sat there like a dumb fool. And now the Wasteland creeps and creeps and soon everything will die!"

With that, she disappeared.

"Was she an evil old witch?" asked the little boy.

"No, no," said Sir Bedivere. "She was just what Parsifal needed at that time. You must learn not to judge by appearances, young man. Off you go now to your home."

Day 13
The Castle of Marvels

THE NEXT DAY THE LITTLE BOY arrived with one black eye and arms full of bruises. "My brother, Skillet," he explained. "He doesn't believe you're a Knight of the Round Table. He said I was a liar. So I biffed him."

"And he biffed you back," Sir Bedivere observed.

"Several times and very hard," said the boy, with a wobbly voice.

"Knights do not cry," said Sir Bedivere.

"No," agreed the boy, with one determined sniff. "Please go on with the story."

FULL OF DESPAIR at having failed in the quest, Parsifal journeyed on without much care where he went. Eventually he came to a forest where he met a kindly old hermit.

"Dear God!" said the hermit, helping the weak knight from his horse.

"Don't speak to me of God," said Parsifal, bitterly.

"Come into my hermitage. You need rest. You need to find your strength again. You must tell me what troubles you."

Parsifal began to tell the old hermit of everything that had happened. He blamed his mother's advice. If he had asked questions at the Castle of the Fisher King, all would now be well.

"Mothers always want the best for their sons," said the hermit. *"But there are stages in the life of a man when he must leave the advice of others behind and turn to another source. Now is the time, Sir Parsifal, to turn to yourself. What are your real questions?"*

Parsifal remained very still. He could feel something

moving within himself. He was getting used to this. But this time it was like a rapid river, rising up from the deepest part of him. The river was full of sweetness, like a nectar, the kind which bees would buzz for. Out of Parsifal's mouth gushed a whole torrent of words.

"*I want to know what the cup is, and what the Light is that is forever outside and yet inside at the same time,*" he said firmly. "*I want to know who the Fisher King is, and why he doesn't die even with a mortal wound.*"

The hermit chuckled. "*Very good,*" he said. "*These are all real questions. Your mother taught you to love; the old knight taught you to fight. Stay now with me and I will teach you wisdom.*"

THE HERMIT TOLD PARSIFAL about the sun, the moon and the stars, and how the planets revolve. He told him how the earth is made out of scent and how the power of love in every drop of water holds families and castles and whole kingdoms together so that they can't fall apart. He told him of the Red Dragon and how it tries to burn up all the waters of the earth, and how the White Dragon keeps making it rain again, over the parts of the land where virtue prevails.

The hermit told Parsifal everything he knew, and then one day he said to him: "*My friend, there is only one more thing to learn, and that is something which no-one can teach, not even the wise.*"

Parsifal was puzzled. "*Tell me more, Master.*"

"*That which is beyond speech, which needs no tongue to speak, but without which no tongue can speak; that can never be taught.*

> *That which is beyond ears, which needs no ears to hear,*
> *but without which no ears can hear; that can never be*
> *taught.*
> *That which is beyond light, which needs no eyes to see it,*
> *but without which no eyes can see; that can never be taught.*
> *That is the Grail you are looking for. Follow the way that*
> *is within your heart and you must surely find it."*

With that, the hermit helped Parsifal on to his horse and
sent him on his way. Parsifal looked back, longingly, not
wishing to say goodbye to this simple hermit, so full of love
and puzzling wisdom. When he got as far as the horizon, he
glanced back one last time.

"No," he gasped, *"it can't be!"* For there, in the distance,
stood the hermit — with a very long pointed beard which he
had not had before. Parsifal's heart filled with joy.

NOW BACK AT CAMELOT the name of Sir Parsifal grew
more and more famous. We heard that every time he met an
evil knight, he seemed to win the battle without even trying.
He killed no-one but gave them mercy and sent them to
serve at the court of King Arthur. Every day another new
knight came in, still reeling from a blow from Parsifal.

One day Sir Gawain thought he would go and look for
Parsifal, and perhaps find the Grail while he was about it.

Sir Gawain was a very handsome knight, with a soft heart.
The ladies used to fall at his feet like ripe pears. He loved all
ladies but was faithful to none.

Anyway, off he went, and as he rode along he whistled
happily, thinking of all the things he would do once he had
found the Grail.

"With something like that under his belt, a man could have anything!" thought Gawain.

He decided he would have a new suit of Italian armour, an Arabian horse, and a great castle with a heated lake. And a wife, of course.

He wanted a wife badly. But he had never met anyone who interested him longer than half-an-hour.

"A wife, yes..." he thought, tying his horse to a tree by a river. He laid down to rest. A wife, that was what he wanted. His eyelids began to close.

THE NEXT THING HE KNEW, a dainty little foot was prodding him in the ribs. He woke up. At least, he thought he did. He could not be sure. For there, before his very eyes, was just the sort of woman he had been dreaming of.

Her face was round, her eyes were pink and her hair was pale green.

"Now she IS interesting," thought Gawain.

What was even more interesting was that she did not fall at his feet like a ripe pear. No, she stood there like a sour apple.

"What are you doing lazing about? Fetch me my horse," she commanded.

Like a servant, Gawain ran off to get her horse. *"Am I awake or am I dreaming?"* he wondered.

The lady made other commands, one thing after another. The more Gawain obeyed her, the more demands she made. The more she demanded, the more his heart beat — boom! boom! By now he was seriously in love. But, oh dear, she was a lady who had never loved anyone but herself.

"Oh fair maiden, what must I do to make you love me?" he asked.

"Love you?" she said haughtily. *"Nothing would make me love you!"*

For the first time in his life, Gawain was at a loss. *"I must be dreaming,"* he thought.

NOW THE LADY LIVED IN A CASTLE. Not an ordinary castle, mind you. It was the Castle of Marvels, on the far side of the river. After she went home, Gawain tried to follow her, but the ferryman refused to take him there, on the specific orders of the lady.

Gawain explained his plight to the ferryman.

"What?" said the old man. *"You're in love with Lady Disdain? Well, you're not the first, not by a long chalk. Everyone's in love with her ladyship, but she loves no-one but herself."*

"What must I do to make her love me?" asked Gawain.

"It is said that if any man can spend one night on the Bed of Marvels, then Lady Disdain will be his."

Now the ferryman had taken rather a liking to poor old Gawain, so he gave him a magic shield. *"Keep it with you always,"* he said, and directed the grateful knight to the nearest bridge.

Sir Gawain tramped downstream. *"Some bridge!"* he muttered when he saw it. For it was as thin and sharp as the blade of his sword.

He stepped on it. *"OUCH!"* he yelled, as the bridge slashed into his feet, and the river below turned red with his own blood. The poor brave knight — he arrived at the Castle of Marvels crawling like a wounded beast!

Lady Disdain stood at the door and sneered at him.

"Look at you!" she said. *"What a sight!"*

"Can I come into your castle?" asked Gawain.
"Certainly not!" she said, and crashed the door in his face.

GAWAIN SAT THERE, making plans. Later, when the
traders arrived bringing supplies, Gawain crept in unseen
through the castle doors. Up the spiral staircase he went, up
and up and round and round, until he came to a vast room.
It was empty except for an enormous bed, a bed with four
posts made of scaly wood, and with sheets made from the
skins of dead snakes. Gawain threw himself on to it, dog-
tired and more than ready for a nice nap. The ferryman's
shield was just the right size for a pillow.

No sooner had Gawain's eyes closed than the bed began to
heave. HEAVE! — and the bed moved to the right.
HEAVE! — and the bed moved to the left. Gawain clung to
it like it was a raft on a rough sea. Then the bed lifted itself
clean off the floor and flung itself against a wall.

"Gawain..." boomed the wall. *"Let go of the shield..."*

But Gawain held on to it, just as the ferryman had told
him to.

There was a ferocious scratching at the door.

"Who's there?" shouted Gawain. In bounded a lion
roaring, with claws so large that they cast shadows across the
bedroom floor.

Gawain lifted the shield in defence, but the lion's claws
curled right around it and started ripping away at his skin.
With a mighty effort Gawain contracted his body into the
tiniest ball he could make. He took a huge inward breath
and held it for as long as he could, for he knew that if he let
it go, all his limbs would flop out for the lion to eat.

Suddenly the roaring stopped. Gawain waited. And waited.

"*Miaow, miaow.*"

Gawain peeked out from behind the shield. There, in front of him, was the sweetest little kitten.

"*Am I dreaming, or am I awake?*" Gawain wondered.

"*What are you doing here?*" demanded Lady Disdain, standing in the doorway where the lion had been.

"*I thought if I could spend one night in this bed, then you would come to love me.*" Gawain gazed at her and thought how beautifully greenish her cheeks were. He was very in love.

"*This is the bed of the Red Dragon. No-one sleeps in it,*" she said, her proud nose in the air.

"*Well, I intend to,*" said Gawain, and promptly replaced the pillow-shield in a go-to-sleep-fast position.

Lady Disdain was impressed. "*Well, sleep on,*" she said, "*although you'll have the most horrible nightmares.*"

Gawain fell asleep at once. He had no nightmares. Instead he dreamt of Lady Disdain and of how her hair turned red, her eyes turned green and her cheeks turned pink. He dreamt that he reached out to touch her and, as he did so, that she fell BLOP! at his feet, just like a ripe pear.

He dreamt he married her the next day, and took her back to Camelot.

But the next thing he knew, he was on a boat.

The little boy looked exasperated. "Well, did he marry her or didn't he?"

"Yes he did. I met her at Camelot. As sweet as a juicy apple she was, and she doted on Gawain. Of course her master, the Red Dragon, was furious to have lost her. So furious that things were now getting dangerous. So a boat came from the Otherworld, to speed things up a bit. But I'll tell you about that tomorrow."

Day 14
The Grail is found

"WHAT HAPPENED TO PARSIFAL?" the little boy asked Sir Bedivere. "Did he start looking for the Grail again?"

"Parsifal was beginning to realise that the only way to find something is by not looking for it," said Sir Bedivere. "Have you ever tried to find something by not looking for it? How would you begin?"

The boy could not answer.

PARSIFAL HAD NEVER PLANNED to become a Knight at Arthur's Round Table, or to go on the search for the Grail, or to marry a princess. And he had certainly never planned to meet a wise hermit, if it was an old hermit he had met, and not someone else like Merlin, which it most certainly could have been.

Parsifal was learning that, far from being in control of his own destiny, something else was really running the show.

After leaving the hermit, Parsifal turned his horse for Wales and headed home. He hadn't seen his mother for such a long time. As he was riding along, he happened across a very sweet girl, walking the roads alone.

"Dear maiden," said Parsifal. *"Why do you walk alone? It's not safe for young girls."*

"I'm looking for my brother," she said. *"Tell me, Sir Knight, you know someone called Parsifal?"*

"Dindrane!" cried Parsifal, jumping from his horse and taking off his helmet. Here was something else he had not planned!

His sister threw herself at him happily. They sat by the

roadside and talked and talked. Dindrane's news was very sad.

"*Mother died of a broken heart when you left,*" she said. "*And all our lands in Wales are now lost. You will never be King of Wales, as you should be.*"

"*I don't want to be King of Wales,*" said Parsifal sadly. "*Nor do I really want to be a knight of the Round Table. I want only two things. I want to find the Grail again and I want to see my wife Blanche.*"

HE GOT BACK ON HIS HORSE and pulled Dindrane up behind him. Together they set off.

"*Do you have any idea where we should go?*" he asked his sister.

"*You must follow the Way that is written in your heart,*" said Dindrane. "*It has a voice — listen to that.*"

This was the second time he had been told this. So at the next cross-roads, Parsifal sat in silence on his horse. Then, as if by themselves, his hands tugged the reins to the right. Coming to a wood, he heard a voice within himself say: "*Don't go into the wood.*" So they took the longer path, which brought them to the sea.

"*What now?*" asked Parsifal.

"*Ssh,*" said Dindrane. "*Just listen.*"

Parsifal listened. Dindrane listened. The horse pricked up its ears and listened. There was the sound of gulls crying in the sky, and the sound of waves breaking on the beach. Parsifal listened so hard he thought he could hear the fish in the sea breathing.

"*You're listening TOO hard,*" Dindrane whispered in his ear.

So Parsifal relaxed and listened and heard the wind in the grass, the slap of seaweed on the beach and then ... then ...

the sound of a sail boat slooshing through the waters. Closer and closer came the boat. It was made of shells and its sails were made of the finest feathers. At the helm was a very wet-looking lady — the Lady of the Lake.

THE BOAT GENTLY LIFTED on to the shore, and the Lady struggled with a boarding plank. Parsifal ran to help and, once the plank was down, he, Dindrane and the horse, all went on board.

"*I was beginning to think you would never come,*" said the lady. "*So, here is your boat, and you will find a friend in the cabin, although he is asleep and dreaming. Now I bid you farewell.*" With that she went ashore and busied herself poking about in rock-pools, looking for pearls.

The seashell boat turned around, all by itself, and started gently to drift out to sea.

"*Lady!*" Parsifal called. "*Who are you? And where are we going?*"

The lady smiled and called out: "*I am one you never planned to meet, and you are going where you never planned to go. Farewell, happy travellers!*"

The boat sailed over the waters following the coastline of Albion.

Parsifal led Dindrane down into the little cabin. There they found a handsome knight, fast asleep.

"*It's Gawain!*" Parsifal shook his friend awake.

Gawain did not know where he was or who he was or why he was. But he recognised Parsifal.

"*How did I get here?*" he said. "*And where are we going?*"

"*I've no idea,*" said Parsifal. "*The breezes are taking us where they will.*"

"Well this is a rum do," said Gawain and they all went out on deck.

They watched in amazement as the tiller turned, the feathered sails caught the breeze, and the boat headed towards a break in the cliffs where a river ran into the sea. Up the river sailed the boat. Everything in the valleys and on the hills was dead and dry.

"I think we are in Wales," said Gawain.

"We are definitely in the Wasteland," said Parsifal.

THE FARTHER THEY SAILED up the river, the deeper they went into the country, the slower went the boat. With a puff, the wind dropped and the seashell boat just drifted. There was a fisherman on the shore.

"Good man!" called Parsifal. *"Where are we?"*

"Nearly there," called the man. *"Tie up the boat at the next mooring place."*

They did as they were told, moored the boat, and went back to find the fisherman, but there was no-one to be seen.

"This way," said Parsifal confidently.

"This way to where or what?" said Gawain.

"I've no idea," said Parsifal, and led the way through a dry meadow.

"Oh, look!" cried Dindrane, pointing. *"A castle!"*

They ran towards the castle and Parsifal began to shine with happiness. *"This is it!"* he cried. *"The Court of the Fisher King!"* With that he began to run towards it and the others followed. As they came to the gate it opened for them and they went into the courtyard.

"Dinner is in the same place," said a servant passing by. So the three climbed the stairs to the huge banqueting hall. It

was just as before. The sick king was in his bed but all
around him a merry company sat at tables with empty plates
before them. Suddenly the plates began to fill with all
manner of good things.

Parsifal, Dindrane and Gawain sat with their plates empty.

"We have to be very careful here," said Parsifal, *"or we will
get something horrible and have to eat it."* He turned to his
neighbour. *"What are we supposed to do?"* he asked.

"Think of what you would like to eat," said the man.

So Parsifal thought and Dindrane thought and Gawain
thought. Their plates brimmed over. Dindrane had a green,
red and yellow mixed salad, Gawain had his favourite, steak
and chips, and Parsifal had a heap of Yorkshire puddings all
brown and crispy at the edges. They all thought it was the
best food they had ever tasted.

AFTERWARDS Gawain was all for lying back in his chair and having forty winks but Parsifal said no, it would not be right.

"*Listen . . .*" he said.

"*What to?*" asked Gawain.

Suddenly BANG! There was a deafening crash of thunder. It seemed to clap in the hall and then roll out of the windows.

"*Dear God!*" said Gawain.

"*Ssh!*" said Parsifal. "*Look . . . !*"

The air in the hall had turned navy blue. In the deep darkness shone a ray of light. It came out of nowhere. In the light appeared a sword, held by an invisible hand. The golden sword glinted in the light and then passed into the darkness. Next came a spear and from its tip dripped blood.

The sick king groaned loudly at the sight of it.

Then appeared that beautiful maiden dressed all in white. As before, she held out her hands in front of her as if cradling a cup of the most glorious crystal. The Light seemed to be running in and out of the cup, endlessly, a Light coming from beyond all light.

Then Parsifal heard a voice singing:

"This, my faithful servant, is that for which you have been searching.

This is that Light beyond all speech, without which no speech can speak, without which no ear can hear, without which no eye can see.

This is that Light which can never be taught. It is always present, serving all living things.

This is the Grail . . . the Grail . . . the Grail."

The song faded. Parsifal's mouth dropped open. Out came a question: *"What must I do?"*

"You do nothing, my friend," said the voice. *"The Grail does everything. It is the knower of all things."*

Then Parsifal asked another question, a much better question. *"What may I do for the Grail?"*

"Love and serve, love and serve," said the voice, well-pleased. *"Then will it be forever present."*

Suddenly, from behind, there was a great snort of a snore! Parsifal swung around. There was Gawain — fast asleep. He had missed everything!

PARSIFAL'S EYE fell on the Fisher King.

"What ails you, Sire?" he asked.

The king's eyes filled with hope. *"Long ago,"* he said, *"I was wounded by the hallows spear."* He groaned with pain. *"It was a fatal wound, but I could not complete my journey home to the Grail until someone came along who could take my place."*

"What do you mean, Sire, what do you mean?" asked Parsifal.

"The Grail is the home of all hearts," said the Fisher King, *"yet among all the peoples this is scarcely known. He who knows this can go home."*

He smiled at Parsifal. *"You have achieved the Quest. Now you must take my place and serve the Grail always. Never ask it to serve you or else you will lose it. Serve it fully, and you too will come home."*

At that the Fisher King's hair became the colour of leaves in autumn. All the old age dropped from his body.

"Your work has just begun," he said to Parsifal, his voice fading. Then he began to grow transparent. Parsifal could see the wall through him. Then, at last, he could see the king no more.

Just then came the sound of a little bell. *Piiinnng!* And for a moment the Light glowed in the place where the king had been.

Parsifal wondered what he should do next. *"O Holy Grail,"* he prayed. *"To serve you, must I stay here in this castle? Or may I travel to find my wife and to see King Arthur?"*

"Go," said the voice. *"For wherever you are, there will I be also."*

The little boy plucked on Sir Bedivere's sleeve. "What is home?" he asked.

"Home..." said Sir Bedivere dreamily. "Home is where we all come from." Megan jumped on his lap and he stroked her.

"When will you and I get home?" he asked her.

"Miaaow..." said Megan, plaintively.

Lancelot and Gwinhavar

"WHAT WAS KING ARTHUR DOING while the Grail was being found?" asked the little boy, stroking Sir Bedivere's cat.

The cat purred and rolled over on her back.

"There's nothing quite like the sound of your wife purring, is there?" said Sir Bedivere, tickling her tummy. "It's the sweetest sound in creation."

WHILE HIS TRUSTED KNIGHTS were going throughout the land, hunting for the Grail, Arthur was not well. He had a pain in his middle which would just not go away. He was also feeling rather frustrated with being a king. He found it difficult to obey his own law, the one which said: *The King Must Stay at Home.*

With all the best knights away on the quest, life at Camelot was not as exciting as he would have wished. So Arthur studied Latin and Gwinhavar made a tapestry, a tapestry two miles long, which showed all the adventures of the knights of the Round Table.

"I wish I could go and look for the Grail myself," Arthur said one day.

"The King must stay at home," said Gwinhavar. *"While you are here, the people are fearless and happy."*

"There's no reason for you to stay, though, my love," said Arthur. *"If you would like to go out sometimes, you should."*

"I'm only happy when I'm with you," said Gwinhavar, and this pleased Arthur greatly.

"I miss Sir Lancelot, though," she said.

"So do I," said Arthur.

EVEN AS THEY SPOKE, they could hear a fuss outside the hall, with many people running and shouting. A servant ran in. *"Sire!"* he said, *"Sir Lancelot has returned!"*

The king and queen went out to greet their friend. He rode over the drawbridge, shining, silvery and splendid, a white pennon fluttering from his spear. All Camelot rejoiced: the best of the knights was back.

To celebrate, we had a feast. Lancelot sat between the king and queen and told us of his adventures. I loved his stories about the battles, particularly one of how he captured the castle of the wicked king of Northumberland and brought peace and happiness throughout that part of the land.

"The castle is a bonny place — I would like to think of it as home," said Lancelot.

"Then it is yours," said Arthur, but he felt sad because once, long ago by the lake in France, Lancelot had said: *"There are many castles in the world, but there is only one King Arthur."*

"What will you call your castle?" Arthur asked.

"Joyful Turrets," said Lancelot.

"And will you have a wife in this home of yours?" asked Queen Gwinhavar, stiffly.

"No, my lady," said Lancelot with a sweet smile. *"Of course not. Did I not vow, the day I became your champion, never to marry while you should live?"*

Gwinhavar was very pleased that he had remembered this pledge.

AS THIS CONVERSATION was taking place I was standing at the back of the hall, ready to serve the ale. Queen Morgana was close by.

"Weasel words!" she hissed in my ear. *"He already has a wife, and a baby son. Lancelot is telling lies."*

"My lady," I said. *"You have the tongue of a snake!"*

"How dare you, knight, speak to a queen like that!" She turned and glared at me till my stomach started to sizzle like a sausage in a fire.

"But tell me, Lancelot," Arthur was saying. *"What of the Grail?"*

Lancelot flinched. It was a quick flinch, hardly noticeable. He soon recovered his smiles. *"I have searched throughout Britain, Sire, but have not found it. I beg your permission to go in search of it again. I cannot rest until I find it."*

"He's a liar!" Morgana hissed again in my ear.

"It is too long since we last saw you," said Arthur. *"You must stay here for at least a month and keep us company."*

Lancelot bowed his head but, when he straightened up again, he looked troubled.

"What is it?" asked Arthur. *"What is the matter?"*

"Would you say, Sire, that I am the best knight, the strongest in arms, the most brave and the most courteous?"

"Without doubt that is what you are," said Arthur.

"Well, what is the point of being the best, if I cannot find the most important thing?" he said.

"Lancelot," said Arthur kindly. *"If you are successful at so many things, why must you be successful in everything? It is enough that someone finds the Grail. It doesn't have to be you."*

Lancelot gazed at his friend. *"You are right, Sire,"* he said, *"as always."*

I studied the two of them. They loved each other, they admired each other, and they longed for the qualities of each other. Arthur wanted to be as strong as Lancelot and Lancelot wanted to be as true as the king.

"Now Lancelot," said King Arthur, clapping his friend on the shoulder. *"While you are here, there is something you can do for me. Gwinhavar has been working too hard on her tapestry. Please take her out riding."*

Gwinhavar was thrilled. She was a good horsewoman and loved to gallop through the forest rides with Lancelot at her side. She loved Arthur as her lord and husband; Lancelot she loved as her brother, a most handsome, brave, exciting brother.

I WATCHED THEM RIDE OFF, straight into a gallop, with Gwinhavar's laughter floating back on the air.

Morgana joined me. *"You should go with them,"* she said.

"Why?" I asked.

"Lancelot is not to be trusted," she said.

"Forgive me for saying so, lady," I said, *"but your speech is poisonous."*

"You're confusing me with Gwinhavar," said Morgana. *"She is the poisonous one. Just you wait, then you'll see."*

I was so upset by these lies that I wanted to go and tell Arthur what had happened. But should I trouble him with repeating poisonous gossip? I decided not to. That was a big mistake. One should always tell the king everything.

Now it was the breath of the Red Dragon that was infecting Morgana's speech, and it would not rest. Morgana made it her business to seek out the weakest knights at court, sidle up to them and pour her venomous words into their ears.

"Lancelot and Gwinhavar are alone, and the king doesn't know," she hissed in one direction.

"*Have you noticed how happy Gwinhavar is, and how unhappy the king looks, since Lancelot came back?*" she hissed in another direction.

Soon, the whole court was awash with gossip.

Now I did what I could to stop this malice from spreading, but once one drop of poison falls from one tongue to another it spreads faster than a plague. I knew I must do something, but I didn't know what.

Then one day I found myself alone with Lancelot. He suspected nothing.

"*Bedivere, my good friend,*" he said. "*At last we have some time to ourselves to catch up. Why are you looking so forlorn and troubled?*"

"*My beloved brother in arms,*" I said. "*The tongues are wagging over you and Queen Gwinhavar. Morgana has poisoned*

*the waters of life in this place with gossip about your affections
for the queen. She says you love the queen and want her for
yourself."*

Lancelot was stunned. In his time he had faced the most
fierce of evil knights, but never had he felt like this.

His whole stomach turned, as if to be sick. He regained
his quiet, and put his hand on my shoulder.

*"Bedivere, just hearing of such poison in Camelot weakens me.
My love for our king and queen is pure."* He then turned,
gaining strength as he spoke: *"I must go away, for to stay and
defend my good name will only bring much distress to those I love
most."*

And so he prepared to leave Camelot quietly, without
telling anyone. Before he left, he handed me a letter to give
to Queen Gwinhavar.

When Arthur heard that Lancelot had left, the light went
out of his eyes and he returned solemnly to his studies.
When Gwinhavar heard that Lancelot had left, without
saying goodbye, she stood and cried. Many people saw her
tears, and they decided that the gossip must have been true,
after all.

I presented Lancelot's letter to the queen and she read it
out loud for Arthur and I to hear.

"My dearest lady," it said. *"Forgive me for leaving you. I
must continue my quest for the Grail. Remember that I am your
champion and your protector. If you ever need me, just call my
name."*

Tears poured down her cheeks. Arthur comforted her.

NOW, ARTHUR AND GWINHAVAR had no children of

their own, but a child had grown up in the court. He was the son of Morgana, Mordred by name. As a child he had played with the king and queen and filled their home with a child's laughter. Now he was growing into a young man and, as Gwinhavar started to leave the hall, he entered.

He was a friendly young man who liked sports and parties. But there was always something about him which I was not sure of. Gwinhavar's tears had brought tears to my own eyes, and I was rubbing them when Mordred entered. It must have triggered that potion which Merlin once put into them, for suddenly I saw that all Mordred's smiles and good graces were a mask. The real face behind it was cold, watchful and calculating.

"*Madam,*" he said, falling graciously on one knee before her. "*I know I am nothing like Lancelot...*"

"*Oh, Mordred, my dear,*" said Gwinhavar, having regained her regal composure. "*You are strong and you are handsome. Be patient. One day you will be like Lancelot.*"

"*Perhaps,*" said Mordred. "*But I will never have your love as he does.*"

"*I love you as if you were my nephew. You are the grandson of Uther Pendragon and as royal as the king and I. There is no need for you to want to be like Lancelot. You are a prince.*"

"*Madam,*" said Mordred. "*Let me take Lancelot's place in his absence. If you wish to ride in the woods, I will go with you. And if you ever need a champion, please think of me.*"

Gwinhavar smiled. Mordred was only fifteen. But she treated him with grace and thanked him for his offer.

That night, when I went to bed, it took a long time to get to sleep. When I did, I had powerful nightmares. I could hear voices whispering, horrible voices, telling lies. Then I saw Camelot start to crumble. There was a roaring sound, the walls began to fall, and the Round Table broke and crashed to the ground. Then out of the rubble came the head of something huge, monstrous, red and scaly.

"The Red Dragon!" said the little boy.

"It's everywhere," said Sir Bedivere. "But, happily for us, so is the White Dragon. So there is no need for you to have nightmares."

The Grail at Camelot

"WHAT HAPPENED TO THE GRAIL?" asked the little boy.

"Ah, I've been coming to that," said Sir Bedivere. "You see, there was something in that law which said that the king must stay at home which Arthur did not understand, but which Parsifal now did. To be the guardian of something, whether it is a kingdom or the Holy Grail, requires you to be at your real home, which does not necessarily mean in a house. It means to be at peace with yourself. While Arthur remained stuck at Camelot, Parsifal was now travelling. The first thing he did was to go and find his wife, Blanche, but let me tell you the story as it came to us."

ONE DAY AT DAWN the air became particularly fresh and sweet. And when the sun rose, it made everything look new. That day there was a great change in Arthur. You remember how pale he had been looking? Well, on this day, the colour came back to his cheeks and at last he was well again. The winter was over and news began to arrive of the withdrawal of the Wasteland. Across the countryside we could smell the sweet breath of the White Dragon.

I went down to the well beneath the castle and found that pure waters were flowing again. I also noticed that blood was no longer dripping from the ceiling into the well. I went up to the special chamber where the hallows spear was kept. It was clean of blood! The crystal shone and shimmered in the spring sunshine and now I could see the spear for what it was, a holy, magical thing which brought health and goodness to the land. I sent a page to bring King Arthur to the chamber and, when the King arrived, he fell on his knees in awe before the spear. I joined him there.

"*Bedivere,*" he said. "*We now have two of the treasures of Britain, and I suspect the third has been found. All our troubles are over!*"

As he spoke, I heard the swish of a silk gown. Morgana was passing by the door of the chamber and, for a moment, her snakish eyes took in the scene and narrowed meanly.

A FEW DAYS LATER, Gawain returned to court with his new wife. She was so sweet, with lips like cherries, eyes like plums, and a skin like peaches and cream. We all liked her at once.

We gathered at the Round Table to hear Gawain's news. He told us how he had met his wife, how cruel and haughty she had been, and how he had won her heart by surviving a night on the Bed of Marvels. Arthur so liked the story, he had Gawain tell it again.

"*The power of Love is a mighty power,*" said Arthur, "*if it can make a faithful man out of you, and a loving wife out of Lady Disdain. This is the best love story I have heard at this table.*"

"*And what of you, Bedivere?*" said Gawain. "*Are you not married yet?*"

I blushed and said that I wasn't interested in ladies.

"*We're working on him,*" said Arthur. "*I'm looking for a good wife for my most faithful servant.*"

At that, Megan jumped on to the table and sat there fixing King Arthur with a jealous gaze.

"*Get down!*" said Arthur. "*No cats on the Round Table!*"

Megan did not get down. She walked up my arm and sat on my head, and still fixed Arthur with her gaze.

Well, a cat may look at a king, but it was such a gaze that the king quickly changed the subject.

"*Now, Sir Gawain,*" he said. "*What of your quest? Have you found the Holy Grail?*"

"*Isn't it enough that I've found a good wife?*" said Gawain.

"*No, it isn't,*" said Arthur.

"*I have failed in the quest, Sire,*" Gawain admitted. "*I have not found the Grail, although I did dream about it recently.*" And he told the story of falling asleep and dreaming that he woke up on a boat with Parsifal and Dindrane.

"*Are you sure it was a dream?*" said Arthur.

"*I'm certain, Sire,*" said Gawain. "*When I really did wake up, there was no castle, no Fisher King, no Grail, no Parsifal and no Dindrane. But it was a wonderful dream.*"

Arthur looked at Gawain narrowly. "*I don't think it was a dream,*" he said. "*I believe that the Grail has been found. Call all the knights back.*"

So we sent out messengers across Britain to tell all the knights to return to Camelot. Many soon arrived, including Sir Lancelot. But there was one who did not arrive immediately, and that was Sir Parsifal.

The little boy interrupted Sir Bedivere: "Had Sir Gawain only dreamt about seeing the Grail?"

"No, he had only dreamt that he was dreaming," said Sir Bedivere. "Just as now he was dreaming that he was awake. That Bed of Marvels can play havoc with a man's sense of things."

The little boy was bemused but asked the knight if he would please continue with the tale.

GWINHAVAR ALSO BELIEVED that the Grail had been found. She had the servants clean Camelot from wall to wall and from basement to spire. There was to be not so much as a speck of dust left. While they worked, she continued with her tapestry. It was almost finished. Just as she was stitching the last hair on the tail of a horse that was bearing its radiant rider to Camelot, a fanfare of trumpets sounded.

"My lady," said a servant, running in. *"Sir Parsifal has returned."*

Gwinhavar fetched Arthur and together they went down to the courtyard. With Parsifal was a beautiful young woman dressed all in white.

"This is my wife, Blanche," said Parsifal. *"She has left her own lands to be with me in your service."*

Gwinhavar liked Blanche immediately and took her away to refresh herself after the journey. Parsifal also went to wash and rest before the big feast. Queen Gwinhavar went to the kitchens to supervise the banquet herself, for she wanted it to be the best ever served in Camelot.

AT THE TABLE THAT EVENING, Arthur was impatient to hear Parsifal's news and, before the food had been served, the king called on the knight to tell of his quest.

"Did you find it, Parsifal?" Arthur asked, coming straight to the point.

Parsifal did not answer. He simply smiled and closed his eyes. Then all the doors in the hall closed as if by themselves. The air grew quiet, there came the sound of little bells tinkling, and the sweet scent of hyacinths.

Gradually, in the midst of the hall, a sword appeared. It was Excalibur in its true form, the Sword of Sovereignty. After the sword came the hallows spear, clean and bright. Arthur's complexion filled out with warmth and sunshine.

Then came the beautiful maiden, hands cupped in front of her. Whatever she was holding had no physical form. From this lotus shape inside her hands poured forth Light, a Light coming from beyond all light.

Such light throws shadows. Not ordinary shadows, mind you, but shadows of shapes of all manner of things not to be seen with the naked eye. One such shadow danced on the table before me. It had a very long beard which was wagging with delight.

"Merlin . . . !" I thought.

"Oh, Oh, Oh, Bedivere!" sang the shadow. "Isn't this what we've all wanted for so long? — the Grail at Camelot! But look out, my friend. No-one stays the same in the presence of the Grail!"

I gazed around me. King Arthur turned into a radiant being, all a-flame with the colour of fire shining in his hair. Kay fell backwards as if some force had punched him hard on the jaw. One knight ran in circles, bellowing and holding his ears. Gawain — dear Gawain — he had entered the most deep and blissful sleep he had ever known.

But it was Lancelot who caused me concern. His face was looking screwed and tortured.

The maiden with the cup of light passed through the walls and we all returned to normal. Well, come to think of it, you couldn't say normal. Well, not in the normal sense of the word.

Kay had a new humility about him, all the pride and arrogance had gone. The knight with sore ears confessed that he kept boxing people, and promised never to do it again. King Arthur seemed to be sitting on an inner throne which could not be moved. He had found his home. And even I changed. I decided that, after all, I wanted to be married. As for Gawain, he stayed blissfully asleep. There was not a dream in sight.

Only Lancelot seemed no different. When I went up to him to check his spirits, he brushed me aside and strode off. He left Camelot immediately.

WE WERE ALL SO FULL of what had just happened that none of us really wanted to eat, but King Arthur desired a banquet fit for a Sovereign Light and the servants were commanded to serve dinner. On my plate was put the largest, most juicy and delicious pear.

Megan, who had remained on my head all this time, leapt down and batted the pear from my plate with a very rude swipe of her paw.

"*Megan!*" I said sharply, and clipped her round the ear.
She cried in protest. The pear had rolled across the table, so I
picked some cherries and returned to the excited
conversation all around. Next to me was a knight called Sir
Patrick. Not thinking what he was doing, he reached out
and picked up the pear which had rolled close to his plate.
Megan miaowed piercingly, and again King Arthur ordered
her to get down, only even more sternly this time.

Sir Patrick sized up the pear, put his large white teeth
around it, and chomped. Within moments he reared up from
his seat.

"*Poison!*" he croaked, clutching his throat. "*I've been
poisoned!*"

He slumped dead in my lap, his eyes starting from his
head.

The hall filled with a great commotion. I leapt to my feet,
demanding to know who had done this. For the pear had
been meant for me.

King Arthur arose. He was quite still within himself, and
full of sovereignty. He pointed to Sir Kay, who was still
nursing a bruised chin. "*Sir Kay,*" he said resoundingly.
"*You are the Steward of the Household. Did you supervise supper
tonight?*"

"*No, Sire!*" he said.

"*Then who did?*" Arthur demanded of him.

"*Please don't ask me, Sire!*" said Kay, full of fear.

"*As you are a true knight, speak the truth!*" said Arthur.

"*It was the queen, Sire. She took my place, in honour of Sir
Parsifal.*"

Queen Gwinhavar looked at her husband in horror.

Arthur looked terrible, but he above all people had to obey

his own laws. *"Sir Bedivere,"* he said to me, his voice strained with emotion. *"You were the intended victim. Do you stand accuser to my wife?"*

"Of course not!" I cried.

But other knights began to storm and shout: *"You must, Bedivere! You must!"*

But why should I accuse my queen, when I was so very sure that the pear had been poisoned by someone else?

Sir Bedivere stopped his tale suddenly when he caught sight of a tall, thin boy. He was standing close by the willow tree, watching the two with cruel eyes.

"I'd better see you home," Sir Bedivere said to the little boy.

"There's no need," said the boy. "It's only my brother, Skillet."

Day 17
The trial of Gwinhavar

"EXCUSE ME, SIR," said an old man to Sir Bedivere. "I believe you are a knight."

"So I am," said Sir Bedivere. "A knight of the Round Table."

"Then could you help us?"

With the man were several other old men. They had bowed legs and bent backs. "We're from the allotments," said the old man. "And all our tools have been stolen. We are not rich men, and now we have no spades and forks to do our digging with."

"Who has done this?" asked Sir Bedivere.

"That lad Skillet and his friends," said another old man. "We haven't proof so the police can't help, but we know who it is all right."

"Yes, very well," said Sir Bedivere. "I will help."

"What should we do?" asked the old men.

"Nothing hasty," said Sir Bedivere. "Let me think about it."

The old men went away satisfied as the little boy arrived.

"What happened to Gwinhavar?" the boy asked. "Surely Arthur didn't let her go on trial?"

ARTHUR WAS THE KING, and had to abide by his own laws. Now one of his laws was taken from the Bible, and it said: *"Thou shalt not murder."* Anyone accused of murder had to go on trial. I refused to accuse the queen, but a knight called Sir Agravaine made the accusation in my stead, for Sir Patrick had been his brother. So the queen had to go to trial.

"Who was the judge, and who were the jury?" asked the boy.

138

WE DID NOT CONDUCT OUR TRIALS the way you do. We had trial by combat. So the tournament ground beyond the walls of Camelot was prepared for the contest between two knights — the accuser of the queen and the champion of the queen. The tournament ground, usually bedecked with colourful flags and pennants, was draped in two colours only, red and white, and was turned into a court of justice.

In the absence of Sir Lancelot, however, the queen had no champion to do battle with the accuser. I offered to take Lancelot's place, but Arthur said kindly that, as I had been the intended victim, I could not act as champion of the accused.

Then the boy Mordred stepped forward. *"Sire,"* he said. *"I beg you to let me be the queen's champion."* Now without doubt there would have been laughter at this suggestion but Queen Morgana gazed about with a piercing look which just DARED anyone to object. She positively fixed Arthur with that look, and I saw him falter in his resolve.

"Very well," said the King. *"Mordred will take the place of Sir Lancelot."*

Poor King Arthur! What he would have given to ride to his own wife's defence, but his laws would not allow it. He had to take his place in the stands at the tournament field, and watch what happened without interfering. My heart reached out to him.

THE OUTCOME OF THE BATTLE would determine Gwinhavar's fate. If Mordred won, she would be found innocent and set free. But if Agravaine won, she would be burnt at the stake! Before the trial, she went to the chapel to pray and make peace with God, but instead of thinking of God, she thought only of Sir Lancelot.

"*Lancelot!*" she cried out loud. "*I need you now!*"

When she left the chapel, she was taken to the tournament field where a great stake had been rammed into the ground and around it a great heap of logs and sticks had been built up to make a fire. My poor queen, she was tied to that dreadful stake, and a man stood by with a blazing torch.

I buried my head in my arms and prayed. "*Dear God, send help! Merlin — can you hear me? Send help! Oh, Goddess of the Land, save your daughter!*"

Though Mordred was only a boy, he fought hard and bravely, keeping to his horse a good long time. But eventually Sir Agravaine gave Mordred's shield such a dreadful blow that boy and horse went down together. His poor horse had broken its leg and was bellowing in agony, but Mordred leapt up ready to meet Agravaine with swords. They clanged together a good long while, but Mordred was weakening. Then came a mighty blow from Agravaine and Mordred fell.

"*Lancelot!*" cried the queen in fright. Even as she cried, a knight rode from the woods, brandishing his spear.

We all grew excited then, seeing Lancelot arrive. We expected him to take the field in Mordred's place. But he did nothing of the kind.

He wheeled his horse below the stands in which the king sat.

"*What kind of man are you?*" he demanded of the King, "*to sit by and let a mere boy take your place? What kind of king are you, that would let his queen burn at the stake like a witch? I despise you, Arthur!*"

With that, he rode to Gwinhavar, cut her bonds and pulled her up on to the saddle in front of him.

"Arthur, you do not deserve such a wife!" shouted Lancelot, and, spurring his horse into a gallop, he raced back towards the woods.

Well, to be honest, this was more than I could cope with, so I went down to the field to look after the poor horse. There was nothing I could do for it, so I had to put it to sleep. My heart cried out in sorrow for Arthur. By keeping to his laws, he had lost both his wife and his best friend.

"He should have broken his laws!" said the boy. "He made them, so he could break them."

"Laws are made in heaven," said Sir Bedivere. "Kings merely write them down and enforce them. Arthur had done exactly what he should have done, but afterwards we could not console him."

"Was it Gwinhavar who tried to kill you?" asked the boy. "Or was it that poisonous Morgana?"

"Of course it was Morgana. I had no proof but her motive was obvious. I was not in her power and so she wanted rid of me. She also wanted rid of Arthur. As plans go, hers was going very well. After this, the court was split in two: half of the knights supported Arthur and the other half supported Lancelot."

"What happened next?" the boy asked.

"The only thing that could happen next: war."

CAMELOT WAS IN TURMOIL, with everyone wondering what side they should be on. In the end, we all followed our hearts. I stayed with the king, of course, and so did Kay, Mordred and Gawain. Agravaine and Tristan went to Lancelot. So it went on all day long, with friendships and brotherhoods being ripped and torn in two. Finally there was but one man left.

"Sir Parsifal," said King Arthur. *"Will you go or stay?"*

"Neither, Sire," said Parsifal. His face was full of concern and he turned towards Arthur and knelt on one knee with his head bowed.

"I beg you, Sire, to remove knighthood from me. I am now the Guardian of the Grail. My duty is to support all and to love all, for all are held by the spirit of the Grail, in equality and truth. With your blessing, O king of all this land, I renounce the forces of war within me."

King Arthur looked at Parsifal. For the first time since Gwinhavar had been taken, Arthur felt some peace within himself. He reached out and placed his right hand gently on to Parsifal's bowed head.

> *"By all that is good and true,*
> *Knighthood I remove from you.*
> *Of the Grail you now must sing,*
> *And be for us the Fisher King."*

Parsifal arose and looked King Arthur straight in the eye. Arthur could not see the form of another man. It was as if he was looking at himself in a mirror.

"*Parsifal,*" said Arthur. "*What must I do in regard to Lancelot?*"

"*You must win back Gwinhavar. Without her, you are not complete, and harmony will not return to the nation.*

> *Go where you must go,*
> *Do what you must do.*
> *Know the Grail within you,*
> *And to thyself be true."*

Parsifal turned to address us all. "*May the Grail shine in your hearts forever, and Britain flourish. May the name of ARTHUR ever be remembered by the Britons and shine like a torch in the darkness. Whenever the Red Dragon reigns over the White Dragon, and the people are oppressed by evil, let the name ARTHUR sound in the nation, and flood the people with strength.*"

Arthur took on the radiance of a mighty king. A surge of power flooded him and, through him, to us all. There was a scent of hyacinths in the air, and a tinkling of bells. Feeling invincible, we put on our armour, mounted our horses, and rode off under the banners of the White Dragon to meet Lancelot in Northumberland.

As Bedivere finished his story, the shadow of a figure fell on the group.

"Oh, hello!" said Sir Bedivere. "Will you join us?"

"What," said Skillet, "and listen to a stupid story? No, I won't."

"What do you want then?" asked the knight.

"I want to know who you are, where you've come from, and what you think you're doing here," said Skillet rudely.

"Skillet!" said the little boy. "Please!"

"You see," said Skillet. "This is my young brother. And every night he comes home with stories about some bloke on the meadow who reckons he's a knight of the Round Table. So my dad told me to come and find out who you are."

Sir Bedivere rose up then, to his full height, which was considerably higher than Skillet. Skillet did not flinch.

"What do you know about the theft of tools from the allotments?" Sir Bedivere asked.

"Are you accusing me of something?" snarled Skillet.

"I am," said Sir Bedivere.

"Where's your proof?" said Skillet.

"I don't need proof," said Sir Bedivere. "Meet me in battle and whether you win or lose will be the proof."

"Oh, don't make me laugh," said Skillet. "Meet you in battle! Who do you think you are?"

Sir Bedivere bore down on Skillet. "I am a knight of the Round Table and Cup-bearer to King Arthur of Britain."

"And I am the Devil himself!" Skillet retorted.

"I don't think so," said Sir Bedivere. "You are just a wretched slave of the Red Dragon."

"Dragon?" exploded Skillet. "I've heard it all now! Dragons!"

Sir Bedivere stared hard into Skillet's eyes, which were as pale as mushroom soup. "If you haven't the courage to meet me in battle," he said, "send someone else."

At this, Skillet laughed shortly. "I'll meet you in battle all right. Name the time."

"When the moon waxes full on the water," said Bedivere.

"And when's that, exactly?"

"In two day's time," said Bedivere. "We will be alone — just you and me."

"Fine," said Skillet. "You'd better get your armour on." With that, he strolled away to join his friends.

The boy jumped up and down with pleasure. "I know he's my brother, but I want *you* to win. You'll beat him easily!"

"Will I?" said Sir Bedivere, thoughtfully. "I'm not so sure. If there is one good thing we can say about Skillet, it is this: he is fearless."

Day 18
The battle at Joyful Turrets

DURING THE NIGHT, sheds on the allotments had been vandalised. Skillet's gang had been busy again.

"Tell me about your brother," said Sir Bedivere to the little boy.

"He frightens everyone," said the boy. "He breaks anything beautiful, he steals from poor people, and he will fight anyone for no reason at all. He has a knife, Sir Bedivere."

Sir Bedivere was not concerned by this and settled down on his stone seat by the river.

NOW I MUST TELL YOU about Lancelot and Gwinhavar and their flight to Joyful Turrets. When Sir Lancelot freed the queen from the stake, she was so relieved that she jumped up on his horse and rode off with him without thinking what she was doing. The further they got from Camelot, however, the more heart-broken she became.

"I can't leave Arthur!" she cried.

"If you stay with him, he will kill you," said Lancelot.

"If you had taken Mordred's place in the battle, I would have been freed by law!" said Gwinhavar.

This was true and the truth of it made Lancelot extremely agitated. *"I was too angry to think,"* he said at last. *"All I could see was you on a bonfire and your husband sitting there doing nothing."*

"He had put all his faith in God," said Gwinhavar. *"So had I. But you, Lancelot, you only believe in yourself."*

Lancelot reined in his horse and spoke to the queen softly. *"Everything I have done,"* he said. *"I have done for you. I am*

146

your champion and your servant. Trust me alone and I will keep you safe. I promise that when Arthur has returned to his senses, then I will take you back to him."

An ease settled upon Gwinhavar. *"Where are we going?"* she asked.

"To my home, Joyful Turrets. It's a great castle and there you shall be safe. If Arthur and his armies should come here, they will not be able to enter until Arthur pledges to live by the laws that he himself has proclaimed for all his peoples."

SO GWINHAVAR AND LANCELOT galloped to Northumberland until, in the distance, they could see the mighty castle. It stood on the cliffs above the sea and had three gates and many pointed turrets. As they rode towards it, they passed many peasants at work, tilling the fields. All the people were delighted to see their lord, Sir Lancelot, returning to them.

"I have grave news for you, my good people," Lancelot called out as he passed by. *"King Arthur has not been true to his own laws and has dishonoured his queen. As I am her champion I have brought her to my home for her own protection."*

The people cheered and cheered.

"Should Arthur make his way here without humility for his grave errors, we shall raise our arms to fight for the virtue of our land and our queen," shouted Lancelot. The people cheered even louder. But Gwinhavar was suddenly very uncertain.

Lancelot turned to her. He could see that she was deeply troubled again.

"Fear not, my lady. It is for your virtue that all this has happened."

She was not very convinced. And if she needed any more

proof that her willingness to go with Lancelot was a mistake, it was not long coming. To the cheers of all his servants, Sir Lancelot rode with the queen through the castle gate and came into the courtyard.

A small boy, no bigger than Lancelot's own boots, ran towards them. *"Father! Father!"* he cried.

"Father?" Gwinhavar turned sharply towards Lancelot. *"Father? You never told me you were a father!"*

Sir Lancelot scooped up the laughing child and kissed him. The boy was the image of his father.

"Well, Sir Lancelot?" demanded the queen. *"What have you to say?"*

All Lancelot's bravery left him. He started to speak faster than the words would tumble out. *"I was on the quest for the Grail and I came to the court of the Fisher King . . ."*

"Yes — what more?" Gwinhavar demanded.

"And I met the king's daughter who put a spell on me . . ."

"Yes — what more?"

"And she laid an enchantment on me, so that I loved her and married her and would do anything she asked," gasped Lancelot.

Gwinhavar was rooted to the spot. *"False and treacherous knight!"* she cried. *"You vowed you would never marry! You have lied in the face of your king and queen!"*

At the sound of all these fierce words, Lancelot's son burst into tears. To add to Sir Lancelot's misery, his wife then rushed across the courtyard to find out what was going on and who this woman was, who was making such a commotion. When she saw it was Queen Gwinhavar, the green serpent of jealousy raged up in her.

"Get that woman out of this place!" shouted Lancelot's wife.

Lancelot did not know which way to turn.

Gwinhavar confronted the shaken knight. *"Lancelot, it is you, not Arthur, who have transgressed the law. It is you who have lied. It is your sweet words of comfort which have been spiced with evil, not those of my husband, who has stood before God and the law for all the people."*

This was too much for Sir Lancelot. He drew himself up to his full height, puffed out his chest, and BELLOWED for everyone to be QUIET. Unable to think of what else to do, Lancelot ordered his guards to take both women to different ends of the castle and to lock them away for their own safety.

He was left alone with his sobbing son. Lancelot sat with him, soothing him, while he pondered events. In his heart he knew he would have to meet Arthur in war.

MEANWHILE, Arthur had been gathering his armies. Messengers had gone out all over Britain, and many kings of Scotland, Ireland and Wales began to move towards Northumberland. Lancelot also sent out messengers, and just as many kings rallied to his call.

The day came when our armies finally arrived at Joyful Turrets. We set up camp and prepared for battle, but there was no sign of Lancelot.

Battle commenced, between our armies and those which had arrived in support of Lancelot. It was an excellent battle. All the rules of warfare were kept, and knights fought each other one to one, honestly and bravely. Many heads were broken, and so were many hearts, for it was a battle of friend against friend and brother against brother. But all the while that we fought, Lancelot stayed in the castle.

Gawain and Kay were magnificent in the field, cutting

swathes through the enemy. Now Gawain had a brother called Gareth, a young man who had been knighted by Lancelot. This was Gareth's first battle, and he was being asked to fight in opposition to the knight he loved above all others.

The first morning he woke up saying: *"I can't fight. I can't fight. I can't fight against Sir Lancelot!"* But we reminded him of his knightly duty and he mounted his horse and rode out into the field.

The battle was long and hard and many of us grew weary. By the fifth day, Gareth, blinded by dismay and stunned by battle, was wandering lost over the field without either arms or armour.

IT WAS ON THAT DAY that the gates of Joyful Turrets suddenly opened and the most stunning spectacle occurred. There was Lancelot at the head of his own army, which streamed out of three gates at once, all silvery and shining and pouring into the field. The fighting grew furious and Arthur, who had been directing the battle from the camp, now took the lead and outshone us all in strength and valour.

Lancelot grew wild in his anger. He stormed through our armies creating havoc. The dead began to pile up in the field and no-one came away that day who was not bleeding. All around the fields of Joyful Turrets, the ground was turning red. Now there is nothing that the Red Dragon enjoys more than a meal of blood, and it gorged itself full that day.

Arthur surveyed the scene. The knights from both armies had fought with gallantry and honour. But the toll of death and injury was intolerable. A shadow appeared before him. It smiled.

"Remember the words of Parsifal..." The shadow twirled around like smoke. Then it took the shape of a beard. *"Remember..."* it said again.

> *"Go where you must go,*
> *Do what you must do.*
> *Know the Grail within you,*
> *And to thyself be true."*

Arthur raised Excalibur aloft. The mighty blade caught the sun in a blaze of light. Arthur's voice rolled across the field like thunder. *"CEASE BATTLE!"*

The warring stopped, and Arthur called to Lancelot.

"Meet me alone, Sir Lancelot, and put an end to this once and for all!"

Lancelot accepted the challenge and bore down on King Arthur. Arthur sat motionless on his horse. Lancelot lifted his spear and, lunging at Arthur's shield, cracked mightily upon it. Arthur was thrown to the ground.

"Strike back, Sire!" we all shouted.

Arthur did not move.

I dropped to my knees in prayer, and so did many others.

Lancelot stood above Arthur and lifted his sword high for the death blow.

There was a pause.

"Well, Lancelot," said Arthur, removing his helmet. *"Here is my neck. Kill your king."*

The sword slipped slowly from Lancelot's hands. Then Lancelot fell to one knee, his head bowed in remorse.

"Arthur, my lord, my king, my sovereign!" he cried in anguish. *"Forgive my sins. Forgive my foolishness. Forgive my error!"* He clasped Arthur and pulled the king to his feet.

Arthur rested his hand on Lancelot's shoulder.

"These errors, Sir Lancelot, do not belong to you. They are of the Red Dragon. Put yourself before the Grail and become whole and true again."

A mighty cheer went up on the battlefield. Brother sought out brother. Friend sought out friend. Peace descended everywhere and the red fields began turning green again before our very eyes.

WE WERE SLOWLY MAKING our way back towards camp when Gawain rushed up to me.

"Have you seen my brother Gareth?" he asked, anxiously. I had to tell him the news.

"He is dead, Gawain," I said. *"I saw him fall."*

"Dead? But he was unarmed! Who would strike an unarmed boy, a boy as gentle as Gareth?"

I did not want to answer. *"Lancelot,"* I mumbled.

"What did you say?" demanded Gawain.

"Lancelot," I repeated. *"He was blinded by anger, Gawain, and couldn't see what he was doing! Gareth just got in the way. Lancelot didn't see him!"*

The Red Dragon had been very annoyed at the renewal of friendship between Lancelot and Arthur. Now, and by virtue of my own words, it sighed with pleasure and smacked its lips.

"What happened next?" asked the little boy when Sir Bedivere stopped suddenly.

"We shall have to wait until tomorrow to find out," said Sir Bedivere. "And of course tomorrow I must also meet Skillet."

The invasion of the pirates

"AREN'T YOU MEETING SKILLET TODAY?" the little boy asked Sir Bedivere.

"I will meet Skillet when he comes to meet me," said the knight. "I thought I'd better get on with the tale while I can. After all, it may be that Skillet will win."

"Oh, don't be silly!" said the boy.

"What do you know of the future, hmmm?" Sir Bedivere asked him. The boy had to admit that he knew nothing of the future.

Sir Bedivere settled himself down and continued with the tale.

ALBION WAS ALWAYS BEING INVADED by pirates. It was such a rich and beautiful land that the pirates came often to steal things. While we were recovering from the battle at Joyful Turrets, news reached us of a large invasion of Kent.

King Arthur was himself again. He looked forward to going south to deal with the pirates once and for all.

"The pirates will be fierce," he said. *"I must take all my knights with me, including Lancelot. But someone must look after Gwinhavar. Sir Mordred, I am putting the queen into your care. Take her back to Camelot. I have no son of my own. If anything should happen to me, you, Mordred, will become the Pendragon king."*

Well, this was rather a lot for a young lad to take in, and it went straight to Mordred's head. He strutted about the camp, making the lives of his servants totally miserable.

"That young knight needs to be taught a lesson," I said to

Gawain, but Gawain wasn't listening. Ever since Gareth had died, Gawain had been moody and withdrawn.

AT LAST THE CALL CAME to assemble the armies. Half were to go down country by road under the command of Lancelot, and the other half were to go by sea, under the command of Arthur.

Now the pirates were expecting us to arrive by road. They did not expect us by sea. When we landed on the coast of Kent they were taken aback with surprise. Being pirates, they were more like thieves and robbers than warriors, and had never heard of the Art of War or its rules. They did not stop fighting when the sun went down, nor did they meet us one to one. You could be fighting one man, and another would sneak up behind you and try to stab you in the back.

Arthur kept control and frequently brought his men back into formation, but the filthy deeds of the pirates kept forcing us to break ranks.

Sir Kay was fighting two pirates at once, lunging this side and that side with his sword. Another came up behind him and stabbed his horse. Both horse and rider crashed to the ground. The pirates pounced on Sir Kay and stabbed him in the back. I thundered in to avenge the life of my old friend, and his horse, with the lives of at least five pirates. But every time a pirate was knocked down, two sprang up in his place. We were overwhelmed.

Then, and not before time, Lancelot's armies arrived with a flurry of trumpets. Only then did we begin to get the better of the pirates. We put them to flight, back across the sea, back to where they had come from.

"*We've won!*" I cried to Arthur.

"Not yet we haven't," he said. *"To the boats, men, and after those vandals! We will follow them to their own lands and make them slaves of Britain. No-one will dare to invade us again!"*

Arthur sent a message to Sir Mordred at Camelot that, while we were away, he must rule the nation in his place. We crossed the seas to rout the pirates and put all thoughts of invasion out of their minds forever.

ALL THIS TIME, Gawain brooded, and kept away from Lancelot. He could not forgive him for killing Gareth. At last, when we had subdued the pirates, Arthur called us all together for a feast.

"So many of my knights are dead," said the king sadly. *"But we have young warriors who will grow to take their place. Let us feast now, and celebrate our victories."*

We cheered at this, except for Gawain.

"I will not dine with you, Sire," he said. *"Not while that man sits beside you."* He pointed at Sir Lancelot. *"He whose treachery has broken the Round Table."*

Well, this was a challenge, and there was only one thing that could happen next: Lancelot had to meet Gawain in single combat.

They mounted their horses and took up their spears.

"False and traitorous knight!" cried Gawain. *"Murderer of my innocent brother! Come and meet your death!"*

No-one could beat Sir Lancelot, not even Gawain. Before long he was on his back with Sir Lancelot's sword at his throat.

"Submit!" said Lancelot. *"Retract your words and beg for mercy!"*

"I would rather die than do such a thing," Sir Gawain retorted.

Lancelot turned to where Arthur was watching. *"Sire, he will not accept mercy."*

"Grant it to him anyway," Arthur ordered, for he sensed tragedy.

While Lancelot's attention was diverted, Gawain struggled to his feet and lunged again at Lancelot with his sword. In self-defence and furiously, Lancelot struck out. His blade severed a vein in Gawain's neck.

Aghast at what had happened, Lancelot threw his sword aside. *"That's it!"* he cried to King Arthur. *"Never again! Never will I bear arms again! There is a force within me which wrecks my reason and destroys my soul!"* With that, Lancelot bolted from the field and left us.

Gawain lay losing blood fiercely. I ran to him, my heart breaking.

"*Don't die!*" I cried. "*Not you! We've lost everyone now!*"

I bent down to hear as he struggled to speak. "*Tell Lancelot,*" he sighed, "*that I forgive him.*" With that, his breath heaved and his soul departed.

Arthur sat with his head in his hands. He would not be moved. I knelt before him. "*Sire, we have had a great victory here. Britain can wax and prosper now, united under her king and strong against her enemies.*"

"*I have lost everybody,*" he said. "*All my finest knights have gone.*"

"*You still have me,*" I said, although I realised that this was small consolation.

"*Ah, Bedivere . . .*" was all he said.

WE PREPARED TO GO HOME, but news met us on the way. It was the kind of news that makes you bang your ears and ask to hear it again. None of us could believe it: Mordred had made himself the Pendragon king of Britain.

While we were away, Queen Morgana had been hard at her poisonous work. She had sent messengers throughout the country to tell everyone that Arthur had died in battle with the pirates.

Everyone had agreed that her son, Mordred, should be the next Pendragon king. He was, after all, Arthur's own choice. Morgana was delighted. Now she had all that she had ever desired, which was power over Britain.

"*Are you sure the king is dead, Mother?*" asked Mordred.

"*I had the news in a letter from Sir Gawain,*" said Morgana.

"The armies are coming home and, by the time they get here, they want to see you already crowned king."

"What should I do?" asked Mordred.

"The first thing is to win the hearts of the people. They have found it difficult to live under the strict laws of Arthur, so you must take the laws away. No laws, no taxes — that's the way to be a great king. And now," she said, *"I must get busy organising your coronation robes. You will have new arms and armour, Excalibur will be yours in due course, and I think we shall have a new Pendragon pennant."* She showed him a design she had made for the pennant.

"The Red Dragon?" Mordred exclaimed.

"What could be better?" said Morgana, and she went away to organise her sewing ladies to make hundreds of flags of the Red Dragon.

"Mother!" said Mordred before Morgana could leave the hall. *"Shouldn't I have a queen?"*

"You already have one," said Morgana. *"Gwinhavar must be your queen."*

NOW GWINHAVAR HAD SEEN all this activity, and had grown heavy in her heart. *"Return home, my king and lord,"* she said to herself over and over again. *"Come home, Arthur, come home."*

Mordred approached. He was doing his best to look more regal than his youth would allow. *"My queen,"* he said to her. *"Our king, your husband, has died at the hands of ruthless pirates. Your champion, Sir Lancelot, is also dead. In obedience to the will of Arthur, I am now the Pendragon king, and you shall be my wife."*

Gwinhavar was horrified. *"King Arthur is not dead,"* she

said forcefully. *"You have usurped his throne. It is you who are the pirate!"*

Mordred was stunned, but only for a moment. *"How can you be so sure that King Arthur is not dead? My mother has told me of this news. Why should she lie?"*

"Why indeed?" thought Gwinhavar bitterly. For several years now she had suspected her lady-in-waiting of plotting for the throne. Who could it have been but Morgana who had poisoned Sir Patrick with a pear and put the blame on herself?

"My king and lord still lives, because I still live," Gwinhavar said firmly to Mordred. *"While his blood pulses, so does mine. While his heart beats, so does mine."*

"Get your poisonous tongue away from my ears, and the ears of my people!" Mordred shouted. *"Cleanse your heart of Arthur, and prepare to be mine."* He ordered Gwinhavar to be taken away and locked up in her rooms.

Sir Bedivere paused in his tale and was quiet.

"Poor Gawain!" said the little boy. "And Sir Kay!"

Sir Bedivere put his arm round the boy's shoulders.

"It's better for a man to die doing his duty than to live long as a coward. After all, death is not an end . . ."

"What do you mean, Sir Bedivere?" asked the boy, but just then Skillet appeared. He had his friends with him.

"I thought we were going to meet alone," said Sir Bedivere.

Skillet nodded to his friends and they slunk away. Skillet took out a knife.

"Weapons?" said Sir Bedivere.

Skillet said nothing, but twisted the knife in the air.

"I have no weapons," said Sir Bedivere.

"That's your problem," said Skillet.

"Filthy pirate!" called the little boy.

"Send the boy away," said Skillet.

Sir Bedivere nodded to the boy and he retreated across the meadow. From there he watched the battle with huge eyes.

Skillet was slim and agile. He darted in towards Sir Bedivere, thrusting the knife forward. Sir Bedivere backed off. Again Skillet darted forward, and again Sir Bedivere backed off.

"Come on, you coward!" cried Skillet. "Stop running away!"

Sir Bedivere stood his ground then and let Skillet come at him. As the boy lunged in, Bedivere caught his wrist and twisted it hard. Skillet grimaced but made no sound. Bedivere picked up the knife and flung it towards the river where it landed with a splash.

"You owe me," said Skillet.

Sir Bedivere let him go. "Skillet, you are brave and fearless. If only you would turn your strength towards the good."

Skillet spat on the ground. "Good?" he sneered. "Good like those weedy gardeners, growing vegetables? Goodness is weakness."

"It's one thing to be strong," said Sir Bedivere. "To be strong and good is something more."

"Oh, get away!" Skillet protested, and he went off angrily to find his friends. "I'll be back!" he called.

"I'll be ready," said Sir Bedivere.

Day 20
The battle of Camlan

IT WAS QUIET ON THE MEADOW the next day with no sign of Skillet.

"Sir Bedivere," said the little boy. "Yesterday you said that death was not an end."

"I wouldn't be here if it was."

"Have you died then?" asked the boy.

"I've died lots of times. Haven't you?"

"Not that I'm aware of," said the little boy thoughtfully.

The boy wanted to hear more about death but all Sir Bedivere would say was: "If you don't fear death, you fear nothing."

He wanted to get on with the tale. Time was running short. So with Megan on his lap he settled down and continued.

GUARDS TOOK GWINHAVAR AWAY to her chamber. There she remained, quiet and calm, her mind fixed on Arthur. She would not let any other thought enter her head. She felt totally surrounded by Arthur's presence. Then, just as the sun was going down, a shaft of golden light filtered through the slit in the stone wall which served as a window. The golden light crept across the wall and began to flood the chamber. A sweet scent arose, like hyacinths, and she could hear the tinkling of a bell. Then a voice began softly to sing:

> *"The Grail is within you, now that you've seen*
> *That your husband alone is fit to be king,*
> *Go where the Grail shows, follow your heart,*
> *For a wife from her lord can never depart."*

Gwinhavar stood absolutely still, her heart full of that light. Then the door to the chamber opened, but it was not the guard who entered. A young woman came in, disguised as Gwinhavar's maid.

"*Who are you?*" Gwinhavar asked, startled out of her contemplation of Arthur.

"*Hush now, we must not alert the guard, who is sleeping,*" said the maiden. "*My name is Vivian, daughter of the Lady of the Lake. I have been sent to help.*"

"*Who by?*" whispered Gwinhavar.

"*Just as you have Arthur in your heart,*" said the maiden, "*so I have Merlin in mine. He has sent me here to take you to safety.*"

"*Where shall we go?*" asked the queen.

"*To a place on the Other Side,*" said Vivian. "*Arthur will join us there, for the Grail is with him, too. Come now, softly. Let us slip out between this moment and the next.*"

Vivian clasped Gwinhavar by the hand and together they sped through the Castle, between this moment and the next, and no-one saw them go. Outside they found waiting two winged horses. The ladies mounted. The noble steeds neighed and pawed the ground then took off, straight for Avalon, where Gwinhavar and Vivian would await Arthur's coming to the Otherworld.

NOW IN THIS HEAVY, PONDEROUS WORLD of ours, where horses do not fly, it was about another month before Arthur and the rest of us got back to Albion from our work of subduing the pirates. What a sight greeted us! The people were full of ale and were thieving and plundering all over the place. Villages were ruined, the land was untilled, and weeds and thistles overgrew all the roadways. Albion was a mess.

Mordred had heard of our return and had gathered an army. It was led by all the lords and knights who preferred Mordred to Arthur. It was followed by a host of thieves, murderers and vagabonds. They were united in support of the boy-king, for the lawlessness and selfishness which were the marks of his reign were making them rich without having to do any work.

On our side, alas, we had an army much depleted after all the battles abroad with the pirates. And we had no Lancelot. He had gone home to France, we heard, and had retired to a hermitage.

AS WE APPROACHED CAMELOT, we met a young maiden at a well. She was hunched over and, at first sight, looked like an ordinary maid fetching water for her mistress. But Arthur was strangely attracted to her.

"Fair maid," he said. *"You are not who you seem to be. What is your message, and what should we do?"*

Now you could have blown us over. Here was the King of all Britain, asking advice of a peasant maid!

"I am Vivian," she said, turning to him. *"Daughter of the Lady of the Lake."*

I straightened in my saddle, alert and wondering. Wasn't this the maiden which our dear Merlin had once loved? One day he had gone out with her and had never come back, not in his old bodily form. Everyone suspected that the reason for his loss lay with Vivian. What would Arthur do with her?

Vivian knelt before the King. *"Sire,"* she said, *"I was wicked once, and by my foolishness locked Merlin in a cave in another world. But I have made my peace with him, and now he is with me all the time as my guide in this world and the other one. Because of my foolishness, he cannot appear in the flesh, but comes as a shadow which, if you look carefully, is always with you."*

"I have seen his shadow, many times," Arthur agreed.

"Do you forgive me, Sire?" Vivian asked bravely.

Arthur paused for a moment, struggling with himself, for indeed he was very angry with Vivian. Then he said: *"In honour of my laws, you are forgiven."*

Thus freed of her terrible guilt, Vivian stood up.

"I thank you Sire, with all my heart," she said. *"And now I bring you good news. Your queen is safe in the Otherworld, awaiting your return. She escaped there to avoid marriage to Mordred, for she is your devoted wife and faithful lady."*

Although Arthur was sad that Gwinhavar was no longer in this world, he was delighted and relieved to know that he would meet her again, at the given time.

"There is something else," said Vivian. *"Yesterday, when I sat down to write to my mother, an invisible hand took hold of mine and guided my pen. The letter written was addressed to Sir Lancelot at a hermitage in France and it was signed by Sir Gawain. In it Sir Gawain makes his peace with Sir Lancelot and begs him to come to your aid."*

"Have you sent it?" asked Arthur.

"Yesterday, Sire," said Vivian. *"Now you must treat for peace with Mordred, and gain the space of one month to allow time for Lancelot to arrive. Only with Lancelot's help may you win this battle."*

ARTHUR AGREED TO THIS PLAN. He had his army

set up camp by the River Cam, which ran between Camelot and Avalon, and arranged to meet Mordred on the following day.

Arthur had a few of us ride forth with him to make the treaty with Mordred in an open part of the country. As we rode, he told us we were to keep our eyes sharp. *"If any of Mordred's men draws a sword, take it as a sign of treachery and engage at once in war,"* he said.

Mordred! I have never seen a man so changed. Ambition had deformed his face. Greed gripped his mouth and envy made his eyes grim. I shrank back at the sight of him, especially as he was emblazoned with the Red Dragon. How great would be the battle that lay before us!

It took hours for Arthur to persuade Mordred to delay

battle. We, his companions, stood by. All the knights were helmeted, with their proud crests of dragons, leopards, lions and dolphins. I had Megan crouched on my head and I outfaced any of Mordred's men who thought this was funny and wanted to remark on it. Finally the negotiations ended. In return for many rich gifts from Arthur, Mordred agreed to one month of peace.

But there was someone, or something, there on that field much enraged by this delay. Some say it was an adder, but I saw it with my own eyes. A little thing, not a thing to do much harm, you might suppose. Hardly a thing to bring an end to the finest flower of British knighthood. But I saw it for what it was. It was a tiny spit of evil, the size of a lizard — the Red Dragon! It zipped in as if from nowhere and sank its sharp little teeth deep into the heel of one of Mordred's men. The man bellowed in shock and drew his sword without thinking.

"Treachery!" cried our men, seeing the sword drawn, and they drew their swords in immediate response.

"Wait!" I cried, but no-one heard me, for now all men on both sides were drawing their swords and, in the army camps, trumpets were beginning to blow.

THEN IT BEGAN, the fiercest battle that had ever been known in Britain. Spear against spear, sword against sword. We hacked and hewed, this way and that, and heads rolled and limbs were severed. Arthur sat astride his horse, directing the battle, sending this squadron wheeling in this way, and that squadron wheeling in the other way, but each squadron that wheeled in did not wheel out again.

Both sides were losing men in their hundreds. The dead

were piling up and soon it became difficult to ride anywhere. Sometimes in the heat of battle seemingly trivial things can grip a man. There I was, surrounded by fierce enemies, and all I could think of was that I had lost my cat. She had been sitting on my head at the start. Now she had gone.

"Megan! Megan!" I called.

Some of course would say that I had lost my wits, though Megan would say that I was putting first things first. Anyway, my frantic search took me away from the battle and up on a neighbouring hill. The fresh air brought me back to myself and from that vantage point I looked down on carnage. A pile of dead lay in a long, snaking heap, and the heap had bonfires for eyes, and smoke billowed from its head. The Red Dragon! I stood gazing in terror. There were two men on its back, the only two that I could see who were left alive. One was Arthur, the other was Mordred. I spurred my horse then, and galloped down to help my king. But I could not cross that writhing heap.

"Arthur!" I cried. He did not hear me. As he raised Excalibur high to strike Mordred, Mordred drove a spear right through the body of the king. Arthur brought Excalibur down hard and it broke Mordred's head in two. I climbed, scrabbled, tore my way over the dead and dying to reach Arthur.

My eyes filled with a mist. There were tears. Tears of love for Arthur, tears of rage at the Red Dragon. It was only then that I saw a third man, standing serene — not a sight normally seen in the midst of destruction. He was a very familiar figure in white armour, standing untouched by anything that had been going on. It was Parsifal.

Sir Bedivere stopped suddenly.

"What happened then?" cried the boy. "Did Parsifal save Arthur? Did he bring the Grail and make everything better?"

Sir Bedivere shook his head.

"Well?" said the boy. "What did Parsifal do?"

"This is the mystery," said Sir Bedivere. "There are those who are good. There are those who are evil. And there are those who have found the Grail."

He got up then, and walked to the edge of the flooded meadow.

"But what did Parsifal do?" called the boy, running after him.

"He did nothing," said Sir Bedivere. "We'll finish tomorrow."

Last day
Time to go home

IT WAS THE LAST DAY of the school holidays and also the last day of the tale. The little boy ran to the meadow with a heavy heart. He found Sir Bedivere standing by the edge of the flood with Megan sitting on his head.

"Oh, there you are," said the knight.

The boy had brought some chocolate as a thank-you gift to the story-teller. For Megan he had a special tin of cat food.

Megan rubbed herself against the kind boy and purred in gratitude before turning to her meal. Sir Bedivere shared out the chocolate and they sat and nibbled in silence. Finally the boy said, "Why did Parsifal do nothing?"

HE WAS NOT THE PARSIFAL I REMEMBERED. He was almost transparent. I thought if I stuck my hand out, it would have gone straight through him. He said nothing, but smiled at me, the kind of smile which says: *"No matter what you think, no matter what you see, all is well."*

Remembering Arthur, I ran to him. He was dying. He gazed at me through his pain.

"Bedivere," he whispered. *"Take Excalibur and cast it into the lake. Do this for me. Do this for your queen. Do this for your soul."*

I picked up Excalibur. What a majestic sword. I could feel it pulsing in my hands, as if something was happening within the very blade itself. I turned the sword around, so that its sharpest edge was glinting straight in my eye. I grabbed hold of the hilt with both hands and walked, slowly, slowly, towards the edge of the lake of Avalon. As I watched

I saw the blade transform from shining steel to a shaft of light, and within the shaft appeared the Sword of Sovereignty, fine-jewelled and glorious.

How could I throw such a lovely thing away? I hesitated.

My beloved king was bleeding to death. Soon, very soon, I would be left alone with nothing to remember him by, alone in a kingless land. I did what anyone would have done. I hid the sword in some reeds and returned to Arthur.

"Have you done it, Bedivere?" he asked, straining to speak.

"I have, Sire," I said.

"What did you see?"

"Only water, my lord, and a big splash."

"Bedivere!" he gasped. *"Go and throw Excalibur into the lake as I have asked you!"*

Ashamed, I went back to the water's edge and took Excalibur up again. I held it high to throw it, but oh, it was so beautiful! It glinted in the dying light of the sun, and I could see the jewels of the Sword of Sovereignty shining. What would Britain be without this? I thought, and I put it back in the reeds.

I went back to Arthur. He was very weak now.

"Have you done it, Bedivere?"

"I have, Sire," I said.

He looked at me then with a gaze full of pain. It was not the pain of his wound, however, but the pain of betrayal. *"Bedivere,"* he said. *"How could you? How could you break my law and tell a lie, even as I die?"*

I cried out then, and ran to the lake, and took Excalibur up again. But my arm was heavy and the sword was heavy and I had not the strength to do the deed.

Suddenly Parsifal was there before me. *"Bedivere, slay the*

Red Dragon in you! Do as you have been told by your king. His life depends on it."

A whole new strength surged through my body, an energy from elsewhere. I flung the sword high into the air. It turned three times in its arc and, as it came down, hilt first towards the water, the golden Sword of Sovereignty sparkled with a message of hope and renewal.

Just as the sword was about to enter the water, a hand appeared. The most beautiful hand of a glorious goddess. She reached out and caught the hilt. Three times she brandished the sword in the air, then drew it slowly beneath the waters.

"The Goddess of Nature has received the Light," said Parsifal. *"Through her waters, every creature on earth is nourished until they are called home to the Grail."*

IT FELT AS IF EVERYTHING was bursting with life. *"Arthur!"* I cried out. *"Arthur must live!"* Had I not saved him by casting away the sword? I ran back to my king.

Three strange ladies cloaked in green had mysteriously appeared. They were bending over him and lifting him up.

"Is he alive?" I asked, but they ignored me. But one glanced up from under her hood. It was Queen Gwinhavar! The ladies carried the king to the lake, where a stately barge was moored in the reeds. They placed him in it carefully, and then the barge began to move from the reeds, out on to the lake. The sun was setting in the west. The three ladies stood in silence on the barge as it slipped across the misty waters, taking my king away. They were Gwinhavar, Vivian, and another I had never seen before now. More beautiful than a princess, taller than a queen, the very Goddess herself, taking Arthur back as she had first brought him, by boat.

I LOOKED ABOUT, speechless in amazement. There was no-one left. Even Parsifal could not be seen. I was alone. The last knight of Arthur's company, left alone in Britain.

"Arthur!" I shouted to the wind. *"Don't leave me!"*

But then I felt a comforting hand on my shoulder, although I could see no-one, and Parsifal's voice began to sound in my ear.

"Arthur is returning now, to the place from which he came. His duty is done. The Goddess has taken him home."

"So he's not dead?" I asked, my mind reeling.

"Those who find the Grail are allowed to live everywhere, forever. They are not troubled by the Red Dragon, nor are they

dependent on the White Dragon. Those who find the Grail come to a home beyond the world of the dragons."

"*This is marvellous knowledge, Parsifal,*" I said. "*And my heart is at rest. But . . .*"

"*But what?*" Parsifal asked kindly.

"*But,*" I sighed. "*Sir Bedivere is still here, on the shores of Avalon, alone.*"

"*Not quite alone,*" said Parsifal. "*You have done your duty well, my friend. And duty well-done is always rewarded.*" Then through his lips Parsifal made a sound to call a cat.

Megan rushed out of the reeds, as if from nowhere.

"*Oh Megan!*" I gasped. "*I thought I had lost you!*"

But she did not jump purring into my arms as was her wont. No. She turned three times on the ground before me, and as she turned, she grew. And as she grew, she began to sing:

> "*You have kept your word*
> *And cast the sword*
> *Into the Lake of Life.*
> *If you will be my own true lord,*
> *Then I will be your wife.*"

With that, the woman of my dreams appeared. She wore a long white gown and had flowing black hair. But her eyes were the very same eyes which had gazed up at me so often over so many years.

On the wind danced the laughter of Parsifal.

"*A boon, my good friend!*" came his voice. "*Here is your wife from the Otherworld. Together you may come and go, in this world and the other one, as you wish. But remember the Grail. Remember the Grail. Remember the Grail . . .*" His voice faded away.

The little boy had been listening to the tale with his eyes closed. As Sir Bedivere stopped speaking, he opened his eyes.

"Oh!" he said with a start. For sitting on Sir Bedivere's lap was the most beautiful woman, as white and black as Megan had been. Indeed it was Megan, in her true form. She smiled at the boy. "Miaow!" she said, and then laughed with the laugh of tinkling water.

"I must take Bedivere from you now, child," she said. "Forgive me, but it is time we went home."

"Where is home?" said the boy. "I want to come! Is Arthur there? And the Grail? Where is this place?" He fired his questions at the knight and his lady. Oh, there were so many questions! "What happened to Morgana? Did Lancelot ever arrive?"

"Morgana became queen, queen of a ruined nation, where everyone prayed out loud for Arthur to return. Each time that Morgana heard the name of Arthur mentioned, she shrank. She shrank and shrank until one day she shrank away to nothing. As for Lancelot, news of the death of Arthur reached him before he left France. He became a hermit and trained young knights to be good and true."

Suddenly a shadow fell upon them. Not a kindly shadow with a beard, but the long, sharp shadow of Skillet.

"Oh, I am pleased to see you," said Sir Bedivere to the thin young man. "My wife and I were just about to go home, but of course, you and I have unfinished business."

"Dead right we have," snarled Skillet. He lunged straight at Sir Bedivere, trying to catch him off-guard.

Sir Bedivere side-stepped nimbly and Skillet missed him.

"Do you know what I admire in you?" Sir Bedivere asked as Skillet returned to try again.

Now Skillet had never been admired by anyone for anything. He was rather taken aback. "No," he said. "What?"

"I've been thinking about you a lot," said Sir Bedivere. "And just by thinking about you, I've grown rather fond of you. For you are without fear, and that is a glorious quality in a man."

"Is it?" said Skillet, very surprised.

"In fact, it is the prime quality of a knight," said Sir Bedivere. "So I wonder, if you wouldn't mind, just kneeling down?"

Skillet stared at Sir Bedivere. He had a choice: he could either jeer, or he could kneel down and become a knight. For a moment it seemed as if he wasn't going to do anything. Then suddenly he fell on one knee.

Sir Bedivere touched him, now on this shoulder, now on the other, and invested him with knighthood. "Arise, Sir Skillet!"

Skillet arose and in his dead eyes there shone sparks of life.

Sir Bedivere brought the little boy before Sir Skillet. "This young lad needs a brother like you to protect him in his youth, and to raise him up a man. Will you take him as your squire?"

Skillet found himself nodding and saying: "Yes, of course."

The little boy gazed at Sir Bedivere, half in wonder, half in fright.

"You will be safe," said Sir Bedivere. He pointed to the willow tree. "Any time you need me, just give me a call. You too, Sir Skillet. The Otherworld is open to all."

Sir Bedivere put his arm round the waist of his wife. She purred loudly.

"Time to go home, my love," he said.

As he spoke, as if from nowhere came a boat down the river. It passed from the river on to the flooded meadow and crossed to them.

Skillet and his brother helped the knight and his lady on board then pushed the boat out on to the water. The two stood and watched it sail away into the sunset.

Suddenly the boy sniffed. Quickly he drew out his handkerchief, his treasured gift from the knight from elsewhere. He looked at the picture embroidered on the corner but, where once there had been a helmet with a cat on top, now there was something else. It was the picture of a cup, from which flowed Light beyond light . . .

Skillet took it from him gently and looked at it. "How beautiful!" he said. "What is it?"

Then the boy sat down to tell the tale, of a king, some knights, and the Holy Grail.